Content Warning:
- Severe Blood/Violence
- Brief Mention of Racism

MultiMind

This is a work of fiction. Names, characters, places, and incidents either are the product of the author's imagination or are used fictitiously. Any resemblance to actual persons, living or dead, events, or locales is entirely coincidental.

Copyright © 2021 by MultiMind

All rights reserved.
No part of this book may be reproduced or used in any manner without written permission of the copyright owner except for the use of quotations in a book review or proper fair use.
Fragmented M logo is a trademark of MultiMind Publishing.
For more information, e-mail: multimindpublishing@gmail.com

First paperback edition, March 2022
First e-book edition, March 2022
Audiobook edition, March 2022

Cover design by Ejiwa Ebenebe

ISBN 978-1-952860-04-1 (paperback)
ISBN 978-1-952860-06-5 (ebook)
ISBN 978-1-952860-07-2 (audiobook)

Library of Congress Control Number: 2021920523

www.multimindpublishing.com

Dreamer

Chapter I

Ever since she was four or five, Vera always had these lively dreams over and over. Not every night but often enough to feel that way. She would wake up with brushes of leaves in her coily hair, her pajamas covered in dirt, soaked with water, skinned knees, ripped clothes or snow in her pockets. If she dreamt it, she felt it.

Vera learned about her dreams and what they were, Dream Traveling, through her mother Adelia. Adelia always reminded her not to fear, as this was a trait that ran all throughout the Florence family tree. She informed Vera that the trait was much more prevalent during slavery times, even used as a method of escape and sometimes to bring families back together. But now, the trait has just about trailed off. "I guess we're not in so much danger anymore," Adelia assumed. The last known member to show the trait was Adelia's great aunt Addie, who kept a dream journal that was buried with her.

The trait tapered off in recent generations, and eventually became a tale of superstition. Even now, few would believe such a thing could exist, let alone run through their blood. Hence, Adelia instructed Vera to keep the trait between the two of them. That sat fine with Vera; she wasn't too keen on the rest of her family anyways. Cataloged as the weird outcast, Vera rarely got along with anyone besides her mother. The elders thought Vera rebuked her Blackness and all the history they fought for because she liked rock bands and wore spike bracelets. The irony was never lost on Vera that she was accused of "denying her Blackness" by liking rock, a Black-made genre. The younger members regularly scoffed at her and called her "White" or "oreo" because of her diction and gothic interests. When she once showed up to a cookout in a fluffy Victorian skirt, a cousin almost set it aflame and another followed her, asking what storybook she dropped out of. It didn't matter that Vera shared her mother's deep desire for history and knowledge, especially about her heritage. She was an outsider all the same.

To be honest, Vera wasn't very outgoing outside of her family, either. Growing up, she made it a point to stay out of the way and remain hidden. Online and offline, she preferred to be a passing phantom rather than the center of attention. Keeping to herself had always been the safer choice. If no one knew she existed, no one could harm her because she existed.

Instead, she found solace in music. Though she had an expansive palette, Rock was her home. It understood her, made her feel less alone. Less weird, even at her weirdest. Through the years, she had developed quite the collection of albums, posters, shirts and wristbands. Especially of bands that looked a lot more like her. She gravitated to them most.

Adelia could hardly understand her daughter's love for such raucous music but as long as it wasn't drugs or violence, she tried to be at least some version of okay with it. A reluctant but cautious version. Her main focus was her daughter's dream traveling. Adelia had dream traveled only once or twice herself but the trait showed up much stronger in Vera, both for better and for worse.

One night, when Vera was eight, she darted into her mother's bedroom with a terrible limp and rope burns gripped across her throat. Awful, red burns seared into her rose-copper skin; there were even prickles of rough twine among the broken skin. Awash in tears, Vera cried about a horrible nightmare: sent back in time and strung up a tree for a midday picnic lynching. There were men, women and children there, all White, all cheering as if at a show. Some of them wore bleached, pointed hoods. Terrified, Vera said she tried to wrest free from the noose and woke up from the shock of falling. Adelia had always been a difficult person to ruffle and rile but this alarmed her. She swept Vera up in her arms and consoled her suffering daughter. She had a feeling this would happen, Vera's class saw a Civil Rights documentary that day. Adelia kept Vera home the next day to aid her wounds. By mid-morning, they disappeared as Vera napped in her arms during cartoons.

Over time, Vera became better about her dreams, just another part of her life. By the time Vera graduated high school, she had come a bit more out of her shell and even had a few friends, most of them online. Vera decided around the end of high school to hold off continuing her education. Adelia had practically fallen out when she heard the decision. To keep a roof over her head, Vera agreed to take only a year off and get a job during the meantime.

Job procurement wasn't as difficult as Vera had feared, she discovered there was one waiting in the wings for her at her favorite music shop, YinYue: Music Under the Moon. Her boss, Derrick Ma, couldn't have been more excited. He even exclaimed the day she said yes, "I couldn't *wait* for you to be legal so I could snatch you up!– Wait, wait ... that came out wrong." Vera just chuckled and asked when she should start. YinYue wasn't far with connecting bus stops, and nestled in a short row of stores. She had a comfortable full-time job as "inventory clerk" but she was dragged into so many decisions and duties by her boss she felt more like a phantom co-owner.

That was five months ago. This particular day was Tuesday and Vera was doing her usual routine before the store opened at eleven: update the album release board behind the aged check-out counter, which was crusted over with a layer or two of band stickers; change the hanging posters for albums coming out that week (Vera would secretly stash the ones she wanted to keep); shelve the respective albums and check the three practice rooms in the very back for any mess or problems.

Derrick was planted in the same place he always was – never behind the register where he belonged. He either messed with the drum sets at the rear of the store's showroom or the turntables next to the sticker-laden check-out counter as his hard worker buzzed about to get the store up and running.

Thirty-eight going on twenty-two, life was always a party to Derrick. He had a jet-black hair rough shorn around his shoulders, a small goatee and dual snakes tattoos wrapped around his built arms. Black snake on right, red snake on left, with the heads covered by his worn red shirt. Derrick had been running YinYue since 2006, the year he turned twenty-five and wound up with a hefty trust fund. His siblings thought he would blow it on something stupid. They were partially right – Derrick never cared about business and described himself as a "Socialist Anarchist". He only opened YinYue because he wanted to stay surrounded by what he loved and had enough sense to know running a music venue would have been too much brain work. Running a small business was decidedly easier. He was partially right.

Tapping out a steady drum roll on the practice drum pad covering the display snares, Derrick yelled over to

Vera as she minded the shop computer next to the tablet till, "Hey! Don't forget to put on some ambiance music or something!"

Vera paused and looked up, a deadpan expression on her round face. She looked over to her boss and fussed, "I've been runnin' 'round like a chicken with my head cut off - You've just been drumming away!"

"You're on the computer, already!" Derrick shouted back across the store. He expertly twirled a drumstick with his fingers. "Pick something cool! Like Avenged Sevenfold or The–"

"Derrick! It's too *early* for that!" Vera shot back. She checked the time on the computer. The store needed to be ready in twenty minutes. Scrolling through the various playlists stored on the computer, Vera decided, "I'm putting on some psychill and trance. Can you check on the game racks?"

Derrick craned his thick neck to look at the music games section crowded into the front corner of the store, the morning sun bathed over the small selection through the gleaming picture window. There were a couple tester dance pads, a standing rack filled with various rhythm games, tester guitar controllers hanging under the large dual televisions and a stack of product boxes, all displayed in haphazard glory. Vera clicked on the televisions and game demos sang out with vibrant colors. Derrick forgot to turn off the consoles for the weekend, *again*.

The owner shrugged, "Looks good to me."

Vera sighed quietly at the computer. How this place

never went out of business sometimes befuddled her.

Derrick went back to hammering out a muted solo as light music began to waft from above.

Once eleven had struck, Derrick finished with the drums and got behind the register. He was tall and always walked with pride and confidence. He tapped away at the register, a thin tablet encased in a graffitied hard shell. Only a sticker showcasing the store's name sat atop the street art square in the middle. A small card reader stuck out of its audio jack on the side, colored blue, lavender and fuchsia in marker. Vera resided in the storeroom, fixing coffee.

Within minutes, the first customer arrived, except they were hardly ever a customer. It was Rikers, the local hip-hop head still hoping for a shot at greatness, even as he hurtled steadily and quickly to his mid-thirties. He strolled in with a swagger that resembled more of a bravado-filled limp than anything, especially for his small frame. Rikers wore black skinny jeans and an oversized black shirt covered with pictures of money wafting down, all hundreds. His tightly braided hair stuck out at the nape with disheveled curl. His dark cinnamon ears each held a tiny zircon stud that barely glittered. He smelled of honey and spoke with a drag, "Yuh favorite customer is here!"

Derrick greeted warmly, "Rikers, my man! Got new duds for us?"

Rikers guffawed with mocking laughter as he approached the counter and slapped Derrick's outstretched hand, "Ah haaaaa, Bruce Lee got jokes this morning. Maaaaan, my mixes are amazin' an' you know it. Twen'ny-nine downloads offa SoundVapor just this past *week*." He smiled a gold-capped grin.

Derrick stared at the small wire rack nestled between the register and plastic tubs of candy. It was a touch taller than the golden cat statue in front of the register and bits of enamel paint chipped off, clearly second-hand. Taped to the top of the rack was a well-designed card: "Try Some of Our Local Flavors! Only $5". In the middle rack sat all three of Rikers' albums. Enclosed in purple jewel cases, the cover displayed a poorly edited rendition of The Last Supper taking place in a lofty banker's office. Stamped above the holy heads was the title "Love God, Praise Money" in gold, gaudy, diamond-studded letters.

With a flat face, Derrick returned his stare to Rikers, "'Twenty-nine'? That's *amazing*. Because none of these moved at *all* this week. Or last. Or this month, come to think of it. I think I even dusted them once. But twenty-nine? Whatever will Kanye do in the face of such talent and competition? Jay-Z must be *terrified*." He pretended to break down and plead to a bemused Rikers, "Don't hurt them, they both have children and wives!" he choked back a fake tear.

Rikers waved off Derrick's ribbing. "Nah, man, I 'on't be messin' with no Illuminati men. That's how they all be makin' their money."

Vera sauntered out of the storeroom and stepped behind the counter, blowing on a cup of light and sweet coffee. She lamented her unfortunate timing when she spotted Rikers. Just in time for his wild theories. Usually, Rikers would leave after Derrick reamed him but not when he is gathering an audience. Vera stood beside Derrick in moral support – she knew he would eventually call her along as co-sufferer if she didn't.

"Both him *an'* Hova, both workin' for the devil," Rikers continued. "Don't believe me? Why they got all them symbols in their videos?" Rikers clapped with pointed passion, "They. Devil. Worshippin'. *Signs*. That's why Hov be puttin' his hands in the air like that, he doin' the Freemason sign and that's Illuminati alllll right there." Reading the clear, wide-eyed disbelief of Derrick's face, Rikers blathered on, "Yuh 'on't believe me 'cuz you Chinese but she be feelin' me, don't you Vera?"

Vera continued to nurse her cooling coffee, her broad nose hovered over the sweet steam. Hot seat. Great. Muffled by the cup, she began, "Actually ...." She removed the cup to speak clearer, "Where'd you get all this information?"

Pleased to believe he had a rapt listener, Rikers explained, "Baby girl, I saw this thing online 'bout Hov an' his hands an–"

"Wait ...," interrupted Vera, "A random video online? That doesn't sound reliabl "

"Thank you!" Derrick jumped in with elation. "Now you and your rapper-alien crop-circle conspiracies can *go*. It's far too early for this and I haven't even had my coffee yet."

Dejected, Rikers gruffed, "Fine. You 'on't see the New World Order comin'. Don't say I ain't say nothin'."

As Rikers swaggered out, Derrick called after him, "And teach your grandma how to use the computer so she can stop downloading you twenty-nine times!"

Rikers flipped Derrick off in the small parking lot and stormed away.

Vera chuckled as she returned the cup to her lips. She wished she had ice to add, the coffee wasn't cooling fast enough.

Derrick mopped his hair back and asked, "Where do people *come up* with this stuff?"

Sipping her coffee, Vera responded with a shrug. "Crazy people are crazy."

❧

Six hours down and six more to go of Vera's shift. Tuesdays were always twelve-hour shifts, to make up for being closed on Monday. Derrick thought this was a good idea. Vera thought this would be a good idea if Derrick helped out more. Otherwise, Tuesdays felt like suicide runs.

The other four days Vera worked were plain eight hours, with Sunday and Monday off. Though Tuesday can be a killer, she still liked her job and the benefits it came with, including overtime.

Wiping a mottled blue rag over the glass, Vera cleaned the double glass doors. She took extra care to clean the eighth note handles and not knock the business hours off the door. The electronic sign displayed in bright blue:

YinYue: Music Under the Moon
Hours of Business
Sun: 12p – 5p
Mon: Closed
Tues: 11a – 9p
Weds: 11a – 9p
Thurs: 11a – 9p
Fri: 11a – 9p
Sat: 11a – 10p

Customers milled about the store trying out the displays and checking the wares as punk music played overhead. Muffled music and chatter muttered from all three practice rooms, they were booked all day. A small throng of people amassed at the game demo area. A new rhythm game had come out, *Stomp Thunder: World Force*, and everyone wanted a turn on the dance pads. International pop and dance songs from the game intermingled with the shredding guitars and pounding drums overhead.

Vera threw her rag into the weather-beaten, moldy yellow work bucket and moved over to the bulletin board hung between the counter and doors. The board was filled with various community advertisements, some in English, some in Chinese, and a few in other languages. Job postings, childcare programs, health classes and upcoming music shows. Postings older than six months had to be cleared off, as indicated by a small blue dot in the corner, which Derrick would update weekly. If there was a printed date, the posting came down the day after it expired. Should there be any inappropriate postings, those were quickly yanked down. Racist ones were always handed to Derrick, who would stand at the front of the shop, call for the store's attention and proceed to light the posting on fire. He would toss out the smoldering mass and address his audience with a kind and polite, "I do not tolerate this. My store. My rules. Everyone, as you were. Thank you for shopping at YinYue: Music Under the Moon." Those postings were quite rare.

Behind Vera slumped in Viper, an up-and-coming emcee working at the electronics store, Volts, down the road. Her demos sold well at YinYue, especially the EP she just released a couple weeks ago, "Beauty Before Beasts, Vol. 1". She still donned her bright crimson work shirt with an embroidered black plug sat over the store's name in circuit outline over her heart. There were pin pricks under the logo; Viper took her name tag off long ago. Her diamond stitched pleather purse hung in the crook of her elbow, cracks vined around the bottom. She had bone straight hair, perfectly curled at the ends. The bangs were stark white, the remainder of her mane pitch black. Several strands clung to her dark chestnut skin.

Viper's cherry-glossed lips were pursed, the free bus was beyond late again so she walked. There was no incline but the summer weather took a toll on her stroll. Her muted plum platform heels didn't do her any favors, either. She had plain pumpkin seed shoes in her bag but she didn't want to be seen changing shoes on the side of the road, it would look uncouth. Only once she spotted the top of YinYue's sign did a free bus pass her, crowded and over forty-five minutes late. Watching it rumble past her, she silently regretted not switching shoes as soon as she got off the clock.

Clasped by the air conditioned cold, Viper released a heavy sigh. She smeared away a trail of sweat threatening to slip into her dark violet eyes, she didn't feel like trying to take out her contacts for anything. She clodded to the counter and slumped over. She studied the Local Artist rack, only one copy of *Beauty Before Beasts* remained in its yellow jewel case. The cover bore a sharp pink stiletto stepping on the head of a burly, disgusting beast. The title was printed below in plain lettering. She hated pressing albums at home but she loved discovering if any of them sold.

Viper scanned the store. She spotted Derrick on the other side of the store explaining guitar differences to an undecided teenaged buyer. The teen tugged at a bleach-tipped dreadlock as he listened and swayed with indecision. Looking over her shoulder, Viper found Vera working on the bulletin board.

"Heeeey, Vera," Viper greeted with charm. The same charm she always exuded when she had a favor to ask. "Can I sit in the back? I just walked the whole way up her–"

"Well, isn't it the Madam Black Mamba herself!" Derrick marveled as he made his way to her.

Caught by surprise, Viper turned around and shot a

million-watt smile, pinning her sweaty arms close. She would usually greet with a hug but not today.

Derrick stood before her with a brighter grin. "What brings you here, Viper? Your CDs are *flying* off the shelves. The downloads are going like *crazy* on our site since your EP."

Viper hid her satisfied grin with a modest bow of her head. She worked hard for her success but she still didn't know how to take a compliment. A diss or snide remark, she could dismantle with the greatest of ease but kind words were another animal she was still trying to get used to. She cuffed her damp hair behind her ear with a ruby nail but her jabbing feet reminded her to stay on task.

With sweet eyes, she graciously accepted, "Thank you sooooo much but could I chill in y'all's back for a minute so I could sit down and switch shoes? I am *dyin'* right now."

Derrick skimmed Viper over and spotted her towering shoes. With a gentleman's grace, he offered an arm and delighted, "Anything for my *best* seller."

Viper took his arm and together they walked towards the storeroom. She tried to hold her own weight and keep an easy, graceful stride but her aching feet jaunted her flow. Derrick kept strong support so the hobbles weren't so obvious.

"Vera, hold down the fort," directed Derrick over his shoulder.

Vera nodded and picked up her bucket. The bulletin board looked neater, the work bucket was fuller. She dashed up the triplet of red stairs behind the counter and surveyed the store. YinYue sold anything and everything to do with music: instruments, supplies, video games, practice books, practice space, albums, posters, headphones, performance equipment and little knickknacks. Derrick wanted the store to be a one-stop shop for music makers and music lovers. They sold international, they sold local, they sold online. This was how YinYue stayed afloat. They even held in-store shows and signing events from time to time.

Derrick strolled back out with Viper. She was half a head shorter now and comfortable in her dingy pumpkin seeds. Striding like the wind, Viper returned to the counter with Derrick following close behind. She had a confident smile and a firm walk; Derrick had a Cheshire's grin.

"Vera! Tell Viper how much of her stuff sold!" Derrick beamed.

Vera's lips curled into a knowing grin as she started clicking about on the computer. Viper had been a regular for almost as long as Vera. Though, Vera never knew Viper's real name, the emcee wasn't fond of it. "You'll see it on two places: my birth certificate and my tombstone," she used to say. In those two to three years, Viper grew from being just another no-name street rapper to a neighborhood name.

Charts and sales populated the screen. "You sold eleven CDs last week and got forty clicks for download from our site last night," Vera proudly reported. Viper stood astounded. "You're goin' up!" Vera complemented.

Derrick gave a congratulatory clap to Viper's shoulders and joked, "This time next year, you'll be getting mobbed by fans here in this store."

Viper was stunned silent. Her long, manicured hands clasped over her mouth. The flat jewels on her nails glittered in the store light. Every milestone felt massive to her. This is what she passed up college and worked awful retail jobs for, and bit by bit, it was starting to pay off. She could barely find the words.

"I wanted to check my numbers, but ... I had no idea...." Taking a deep breath, she exhaled, "*Wow.*" Her hands dropped down.

Derrick insisted, "You need to bring more CDs in! We're running low a little."

Viper nodded and adjusted her bag, "I'm gonna go now and press some! I'll see y'all tomorrow, bright an' early!" She left the store with a proud bounce in her step.

Still basking in the moment, Derrick praised, "Top earner right there. Works hard, gives no bull, and her music is at least more than half decent. More Vipers, less Rikers." He propped himself against the sales counter and fiddled with the golden lucky cat. A gift from his sister, since she was sure he needed it. Derrick already had rubbed the gold off the top of the raised paw from the many times he's thumbed it.

Vera checked YinYue's social media, "Why do you put up with that dude, man?" The notifications were at normal rates, just a couple questions about their practice rooms sitting in their messages. They had a sizeable following of a few thousand but nothing too stupendous. They were a small business in a small town but they made their online presence seem bigger and it paid off well. Derrick was a mastermind at guessing what would resonate well and when to schedule posts, mostly so he didn't have to remain tethered to the computer all day.

He sighed, "He'll whine if I don't. I've tried."

༄༅

Soon, the day winded down to closing time, the favorite time of day. Vera picked up the store's microphone and announced, "Shoppers and browsers, YinYue is about to close in five minutes. Please bring your purchases to the register now. If you are in the practice rooms, please pack up and take your trash with you. Thank you for shopping at YinYue: Music Under the Moon." The dented microphone whined with a little feedback as she switched it off. Vera cued the vintage farewell serenade to play over the speaker system as customers lined up.

Vera had been behind the counter the entire night as Derrick spent the evening in the storeroom assembling online orders he should have done earlier. He always kept online orders until the last minute – or if he needed an excuse to get away from an annoying customer.

Taping up his final box and slapping a printed label on it, Derrick left from the storeroom to check the practice rooms. Despite the many signs he had on every door of the three practice rooms, still he would find trash and sometimes worse in the soundproofed rooms. The worse dropped off recently since the new cleaning fee (only applied if worse was found) was upgraded to two hundred and fifty dollars and every room had to have a name, email, phone number and paying account attached and prepaid. Coupled with a ban list, Derrick stumbled over far less horrible discoveries. Now, it was picking up the occasional snack wrapper and straightening up the chairs and music stands.

After the last customer filed out, Vera locked the front doors and rolled down the steel window covers. They clanked with a heavy ring as Vera pulled on the dingy, oily chain. She wore the work gloves stored under the till, draped over an aluminum baseball bat.

Behind her, Derrick sauntered through with the work bucket and emptied it into the waste basket behind the counter. The plastic bag crinkled and rustled as the bin filled half-way. The steel cover clinked to a slow finish as Derrick placed the bucket away and checked the till, which blended into the counter and was covered with stickers. It tinged out with a light tap into his stomach. He checked the totals of the day against the till and counted the remaining money. He slipped out a ratty memo pad from under the tablet stand and jotted down the numbers. Under the money rack in the till, he slipped out a clear money bag. Derrick copied the numbers onto the bag and carefully filled the bag. Coins jangled one by one as Vera went into the storeroom for a dust mop. The night was truly uneventful.

As Vera worked on the marble tiled floors of the practice rooms, Derrick triple checked his numbers on the memo pad and scanned the area for any forgotten coins. Satisfied to find nothing under his vigilant eye, he closed the memo pad and slid it back under the tablet stand and then sealed the money bag shut to bring it to the storeroom's safe. It was a classic-looking safe with a grey dial and hidden behind a filled record crate. Derrick pulled aside the record crate, spun in the correct combination and opened the safe with a cold, metal click. The safe's door creaked in pips and long whines.

Inside the empty safe, velvet coated the walls. Derrick grew into the habit of emptying the safe on Sundays after closing. It helped him mentally close out the week. He used to empty the safe when it was full but a close shave changed his mind: Tire, Shocks & More, the auto part store next to YinYue, was struck with a burglary after hours three years ago. He didn't always count the money or get special bags either but time proved a strict teacher. It only took a few miscounts to learn.

Vera walked into the storeroom, dust mop and work bucket in each hand. Her legs ached and her head felt drained. She placed up the mop and bucket against the bathroom wall as Derrick tossed in the money and shut the safe door. She propped herself against the bare cinder block wall and asked, "How'd we do today?"

Giving the dial a hearty spin, Derrick answered over

the whirr, "Still afloat. YinYue lives to see another day." He stood up to stretch his aging knees and back, croaking out, "We're not surfing but we're afloat." A small twinge popped in his neck, he rubbed it. He was young at heart, not in flesh. "Ready to go?"

Vera nodded. Behind her were a set of light switches and an alarm panel next to the scuffed up door. She closed the door, turned off the store lights and set the alarm. Hearing a rhythmic beep, both Vera and Derrick walked through the long storeroom to the giant, heavy double doors waiting for them. The storeroom spanned the entire store's length. There were two bathrooms jutting out the wall, one for Vera and one for Derrick. Old signs, logos and gear lined the hall. Inventory sat on plywood shelves Derrick spent weeks erecting himself when he first bought the store. He was grateful old friends loaned him their tools. His father owned a small chain of hardware stores downtown but scoffed, "Why should I donate to failure? I may as well loan my tools to the Marble Boat. When that sails, then see me."

The duo exited the beat up double doors, wide graffiti spanned the entirety of both sides. Derrick started his beaten up red truck with his key as the alarm continued to beep behind him, eventually silenced by the bang of the doors. His truck was an old clunker but he loved his new wireless key. The headlight bathed them in a bright glow as the truck idled loudly with a terrible rattle. Derrick had tried to fix the engine himself in the past but he only made the rattle worse, especially because it was the exhaust system, not the engine, that caused the problem. Stickers coated the steel back bumper in a thick layer, ranging in theme from politics to music. Some were faded, others were new. Vera liked reading them when she took breaks outside.

With a mechanical pop of the passenger side lock, Derrick unlocked Vera's side first. He sprang down from the loading dock to unlock his side by hand. Vera took her time climbing down the ledge of the loading dock. The grumble of the engine vibrated though her fingertips as she pulled open the handle. She gripped the sides of the doorway and with a strong yank, she hopped onto the passenger seat. The leather was cracked and worn, dirty foam jutted out.

Waiting for Vera to settle in and buckle up, Derrick popped in a thrasher metal CD and turned the volume dial low. He then shifted into reverse, the driving shaft orb covered in black duct tape, backed out and drove away.

The drive was relatively quiet. Drilling music played over the angry jostling in the back seat. So many things filled the back, the truck practically served as a moving storage room. There were jackets, books, even a crate of maintenance supplies such as a windshield scraper and a wrench set.

It was a short ride to Vera's house, just a few blocks. Vera usually got rides home on Tuesdays since she helped close. Otherwise, she'd wait for the free bus. There was a stop in front of YinYue and another half a block away from her home, not much of a challenge.

Derrick pulled up to the small, two-storied house. It laid on flat ground with very little yard or lawn to speak of. The roof had a flat tent and the walls were made of brick. The face of the house was hidden in the moonlight shining behind it. The street lights were out on the block again, third time this season. Lining the yard was a wooden fence with a mismatched iron gate. The gate was a delicate work of tangled roses flowing into an intricate curve. Solar stakes traced up the stone-spotted path from the gate to the black storm door. The storm door also bore latticed flowers in the metal work. The mustard yellow door behind it held a narrow arc window pane deeply aglow – Adelia was home.

Vera waved goodbye to Derrick and pulled on the handle to exit the clunky truck. The grumble of the engine always reminded her of a combine tractor. She slammed the door shut; it never closed with anything less.

"Bye Derrick!" Vera shouted over the engine and walked on to the sidewalk as Derrick pulled off. The thrasher music rocketed up, drowning out the engine.

She dug for her phone as she unhooked the gate and walked through. The gate banged back and re-hooked itself. Traveling up the stone path, her phone lit up her plump face as she checked all that she missed since lunch break. The clock gears in her phone case ticked loosely in her palm with her every step, the gentle discs of light illuminated her scuffed, thick boots.

There was a new update on her favorite online show, *Mystery Pop Pop*. It was a comedic mystery show filled with silly antics and unusual turns. Vera read comments about a surprise twist that leaked as she dug for her keys. She pulled out her keys by the eight-ball keychain and opened the storm door. Screenlight painted her face and the yellow door as she fumbled for the correct key and unlocked the door.

Vera never broke sight with her screen, even as she walked in. She tapped the door shut with her heel. The living room felt cool, and brass table lamps filled the room in a clean glow. It bordered on the cusp of messy, short stacks of books and movie cases dotted around the overcrowded and short bookcase. In the bookcase held the heaviest and widest book in the house, the Encyclopedia Africana. Vera once tried to pick it up, it felt heavier than two bricks. The television sat atop the bookcase, playing an Italian cooking show at medium volume. Adelia sat on the sand gray couch in front of the television, focused on her tablet. She had close cropped, coily jet black hair and dark, cherry-brown skin.

Vera blindly greeted, "'Ey, Ma," and headed up the stairs. She sprang over the first triplet of stairs and landed soundly on the square landing before turning and heading up the rest. They whimpered and whined underfoot, knobby and well past their time.

Adelia acknowledged her daughter with a distracted wave and kept scrolling. She was comparing bulb prices, the back patio light wouldn't stop buzzing or flickering. Home improvement projects gave her something fruitful to do; the job she had as delivery dispatcher head supervisor wasn't cutting it. The only thing she liked about that job was that it kept the lights on and her family fed.

Vera exited the stairs and went down the dark, narrow hall into her room. She used the bask of her phone for light until she turned on her bedroom's lamp. Band posters covered her walls, and a spaceship hung from under the ceiling light. Albums splayed across the top of her squat, plastic dresser. She liked digital music but hated how she couldn't truly "own" the tracks. At least with CDs, she didn't worry about having to buy the same song just to hear it somewhere different or DRM pulls. Like the stairs, the floorboards creaked with her every step. Some of the slats bore deep pockmarks and missing strips.

Her room wasn't small, just crowded. She had a twin bed covered in clothes and albums. Her laptop laid near her black satin pillow, plugged up and asleep. Silver blue drapes and crystal beaded curtains hung over her bed. The closest was half full, the remaining half laid scattered around her room.

Vera bundled the clothes that laid on her bed into a pile, threw the albums on top, placed them on top of the dresser, and flopped down in front of her laptop. Striking orange detail ebbed to life on the lid of the computer as it woke up. The keyboard lit up the same volcanic orange, the laptop whirred softly. Vera kicked off her work boots to better curl up on her bed. It took little time for the episode page for *Mystery Pop Pop* to load. She always had a tab opened to their episode list for convenience.

She dug around behind the laptop to find a cord to plug her phone up with. The sensation around the leaks was at a fever pitch. She hoped the rumors she heard over the past week weren't true, the leaks neither confirmed nor denied them. She heard that her favorite character, Leilani, might be killed off to make way for the second lead, Daymond. It would break Vera's heart if so, Leilani was the only one worth watching but she hadn't been in a couple recent episodes and the season finale was the next one.

The webpage of *Mystery Pop Pop* spared little frill and decadence. The show operated on a shoestring budget but made every penny count. Red curtains lined the borders of the site, and playing cards decorated every episode thumbnail. The season finale was at the top of the list, out a little earlier than usual. Vera brimmed with delight and anticipation. She jumped off the bed, turned off the lights and hopped back on. Rocking from her joyous shockwave, Vera steadied the computer. She stretched out her short, thick legs, slid the laptop onto her lap and clicked "Play".

Chapter II

Morning arrived quickly. Much too quickly.

Vera woke up, bleary and jumbled. A random episode of *Mystery Pop Pop* played on her screen. Little did she know, Vera had fallen into a dreamless slumber twenty minutes into the forty-five minute show. She saw a glimpse of her favorite character, Leilani, before drifting off during an episode flashback.

Checking the time on her computer, Vera blinked hard several times to adjust to the shining sunlight. The day was bright, brilliant and blinding as rays sprawled across her pillow. 9:34 AM, almost a whole hour past when she should have woken up and almost fifteen minutes before her shift would start.

Perked with alarm but still leaden with sleep, Vera scrambled off the bed. She did a quick look-over, at least she still had on her work clothes. Once, she woke up with a warrior gauntlet and a soft fox pelt made of iron. Those lived in the deep corner of her closet. In vain effort to hide the fact she was wearing yesterday's clothes, Vera rooted out a faded, black vest from her clothes pile and threw it on. She yanked her phone from the charger and slipped her work boots back on. With no time to waste, Vera opened her phone and tried to get a quick lift through TwipRide. Everything was on-peak and expensive but she had no other choice, her mother had already driven off to work.

Tapping in her home information because the GPS was too slow to turn on and focus, Vera dashed into the bathroom, narrowly missing a tumble down the stairs during a skidding turn. As she waited for TwipRide to load, Vera brushed her teeth. By the time she washed out her mouth, TwipRide picked her a driver that was four minutes away. A little micro car popped up with the driver's details and picture but Vera swiped it away, all she wanted was a speed demon that could dash her to work in less than twelve minutes. Vera spotted flecks of toothpaste on her cheeks and a wipe of it on her nose. She smeared water all over her lower face and turned off her sink with a squeak. She was all clear during the second check. Her wild cloud of hair bore a flat side from her pillow. Vera picked it out in haste and promised herself to scour YinYue for a rubber band to mask her hasty work. Her phone beeped, the micro car honked its horn and text displayed underneath on the rolling map "Your ride is almost here! Less than a minute away."

Vera gave her face a couple quick pats with the powder blue towels as she pocketed her phone in a side cargo pocket. Then, she ripped out of the bathroom and thundered down the stairs, checking her pockets for keys. The living room was awash with golden daylight as Vera erupted out the front door.

Slamming the door shut, Vera gave her waiting driver a start. Frozen against his window, clutching his heart, the college student watched Vera rocket down the stone path and spear into his car. The sedan rocked a little from her impact; the driver paled a couple shades from his warm mahogany.

Before the driver could thaw, Vera rushed out, "YinYue, please! Forty-five thirty-five Woodson Way!"

Still shocked and wide eyed, the driver pulled himself from the window and started their journey. He said nothing, it was too early to even try. He just wanted this trip to be over and drove like it.

Vera gripped the seat as the car raced down the street. She apologized a little slower as she checked her phone, "Sorry, I'm super late."

It was a mad dash to YinYue; the driver took nothing but hard corners and dangerous shortcuts. Anything to get this frantic client out his car faster. Vera arrived at work with a minute to spare but she was dropped off at the front of the locked business, not the back like she asked when they were close. With no time to argue, Vera jumped out the car and slammed it shut. As the car sped away,

Vera ran up to the front doors and banged on them with an open palm. The gates were up and the lights were on.

A little more banging and Derrick popped out from the storeroom, his phone glued to his ear and a bewildered, confused expression marked on his face. He sauntered up to the door with a calm, bemused stride as he watched Vera wave and point to the lock between the handles. She only had the key to the back, not the front because the only time she used the front doors were for her later shifts.

Derrick pressed the mic of his phone against his shoulder and asked through the glass, "What's the password?" The thick glass muffled his voice.

Vera stomped her foot, "Come on, Derrick! It's too early for that!" Derrick continued his call as Vera yelled, "I just ran up here! We don't have a password!"

Derrick returned the phone to his shoulder. "Yes we do." He returned to his call.

"No, we don't!" Vera protested.

Derrick turned about and started to walk away. Vera banged on the door's window again. She took a quick glance around, she started to feel ridiculous and figured it would only be a matter of time before she'd gather a crowd of some sort. Workers of the surrounding stores were filtering in as well.

Vera shouted, "What's the password! 'Sleeping Beauty'?"

The owner stopped and turned on a booted heel. He drifted back to the doors and clicked the metal latch.

Derrick cracked open the left door and placed the phone against his shoulder. With a simple and gentle tone, he informed, "The password is 'I'm late'."

Vera barreled past him using the other door. "I am *not* late!" she said defiantly as she stormed to the storeroom for a rubber band.

Derrick continued his call, unbothered by her temper. "Nà shì shéi? Vera, tā chídàole."

Vera had heard Derrick as she stormed back out, no rubber band to be found. As she scoured around the shop computer, her ears perked.

Derrick chuckled at the response on the other end, "I know, right?"

Ears burning, Vera darted upright and asked over the computer, irate, "Hey, Derrick! Some help?" Any excuse to make the conversation stop.

Derrick nodded at Vera in acknowledgment. To the person on the other line, he said, "Hey, talk later? Duì, duì. Bye bye," and hung up. He found Vera focused on him with a frying glare. "What?"

Vera accused, "I heard my name. Y'all were talkin' 'bout me!"

Derrick rolled his eyes as he slipped his phone into the back pocket of his black pants, "Christ, Vera, my cousin wanted to know who was in the background. I wasn't rippin' on you in another language."

"You sure?" Vera wasn't convinced.

The owner blew out a defeated sigh and rubbed his face. "Vera, either learn Mandarin or stop worrying about what I say in my personal conversations," he stated firmly.

Vera's fire shriveled. "It's just ...," Vera tried to look for the words but Derrick responded in the trailing silence instead.

"If you want me to talk in English each and every time or each and every mention I make of you just so you can feel better, regardless of what I say, you are very stunningly close to needing a new job." Vera hastily straightened up and stammered but Derrick cut her off quick, "Let me finish: This is *my* business. I can talk in *my* home language to *my* family in *my* store if *I* want to. Especially to relatives who have very poor English, like my cousin. Now," Derrick dropped his hard tone for a sweeter demeanor, "any questions or can I be the wonderful, adorable, fun loving and incredibly handsome boss I always strive to be? Besides, I know where you 'secretly' stash your posters. Twenty points for bucking capitalism, minus fifteen for stealth. I used to snatch cologne and spray paint from the rich stores uptown as a kid. Sneak smarter." He snickered to himself.

Vera stuttered out an apology with her head dropped low and returned to the computer, stewing in awkwardness. She didn't mind that her boss spoke in more than one language, she just didn't want anything bad said about her in any language. She sighed and picked the light music for that morning, Victorian classical.

Soft music in the morning was still quite new for YinYue. If it were up to Derrick, the store would be playing louder and harder genres every moment of the day.

Somehow, Vera managed to reason to Derrick that there was such a thing as "too early" for raging metal and brash punk, especially for the average customer. With the compromise of trying out "Soft Time" only for the summer and up until half past noon, Derrick reluctantly agreed.

Vibrant violins piped out from the overhead speakers as Vera searched the store to find whatever Derrick didn't do for opening. She gave out a gaping yawn as she noticed some of the practice room info boards weren't updated for the day.

❧❦❧

By half past noon, Vera felt beyond ran down. She tapped Derrick as he stood over the shop computer deciding new music and told him she was going to take her half hour break in the storeroom.

Tucked behind the dual bathrooms in the back was a little dusty brown cot situated under a tall shelf. There on that cot sat a travel pillow, a small teddy bear Derrick left "for décor", and, at the foot of the cot, a thin blanket clumped up in a pile. Vera closed the storeroom door and dragged herself to the cot. She fluffed the lumpy pillow and slipped off her shoes to lay down. She normally avoided naps at work because of her dreams but today she was too dragged down to care. Vera pulled out her phone to set an alarm to ring in half an hour and placed it against her leg. Ska blared throughout the store as she sorted to get comfortable, muffled by the cinder block walls and closed door. Once her head touched the pillow, Vera was out.

The dream was simple and pleasant. Vera was sliding down a dense forest path like a snowboarder. Rugged terrain passed beneath her mountain boots like smooth snow. She could feel every pebble and twig. She sliced between evergreens in the cool mountain air as sprigs of needles caught in her hair. The rushing wind turned one cluster of needles into a golden feather fascinator, solid and heavy.

It was exhilarating, until her legs started to sink into the ground as she gained momentum, speeding towards a grassy cliff and the great expanse of the wild blue yonder.

Half-way sunk to her mid calves, Vera leaned back to fall on her hands and rump. She skidded to a stop just before she crossed onto the grassland. Her hands then sank into the ground like quicksand as she started to slide again. Crossing into the grassland, Vera struggled to pull out her hands and stop herself but she was jarred awake with a close hiss and heavy shake.

"Vera! Ver-ron-nic-ca!" Derrick rattled Vera. Concern knitted across his face, he almost shook her like a doll.

"Whaaaaaaaat?" Vera whined. For once, she felt like she was getting in some restful sleep. "I'm on breaaaaaaak," she bumbled out as she picked up her phone with a clumsy grip. She checked the time: Break ended over half an hour ago. Time was *not* on her side today.

"What the *hell* were you *doing*?" Derrick hissed. "Look at you!"

Vera looked down at herself and jumped with a start. Covered in dirt up to her knees and elbows – and caught by her boss, no less.

Bewildered, Derrick blustered, "Viper's watching the store. I heard your phone go off but you never came out. I come in here and here you are with that hair thingy–" Derrick pointed to Vera's gold fascinator, which Vera clasped in shock "- growing out your poof and your pants and your hands were starting to get dirty like you were wading through dirt. I *had* to wake you."

Vera's mind swam. She never planned for this moment, for accidental discovery; every time she thought about it, she just would will the worry away. Now she was silent and petrified.

Derrick gave Vera's shoulder a firm shake, "Vera. Vera, you alright? Talk to me!"

Her jaw bobbled, words refused to come. In the deep ocean of realization, she was drowning. Feeble voiced, she tried to save herself, "I ... I can explain." She stared at Derrick's waiting, worried face. She looked away, shaking her head, "No ... no, I can't."

"Stay here," Derrick ordered. "Don't. Move." He ran back into the store, snapping the storeroom's door shut. Vera could hear a muffled announcement over the loudspeaker, "Everyone, YinYue will be closing early today at two. I sincerely apologize for the inconvenience. YinYue will be closing today at two. Thank you for shopping at

YinYue: Music Under the Moon."

Vera's lips lightly parted, stupefied. The music abruptly changed from thundering thrash to the farewell song. Her phone beeped a quick synth cord. Vera checked, a Twip update from YinYue blipped up on her phone. She tapped it open:

> Due to Family Emergency, YinYue will be closing early today @ 2
> – Derrick, Owner

Beneath the message was the same in Chinese. Numbness prickled throughout Vera. *I'm so screwed*, the thought floated across her mind as her stomach sank. She wanted nothing more than to disappear. Vera then heard Viper by the door. Her voice was rapid, vicious and baffled.

"Boy, you is not makin' *any* sense! Why you ain't tryna tell me nothin'? Why can't I see her-"

"Viper, *please*," Derrick begged. He sounded closer to the door, most likely trying to keep it closed. The knob struggled for a moment. "Tomorrow! I *promise* to tell you everything *tomorrow*. I can't talk about this now-"

"If you don't *move*-"

"Viper, she will be here *tomorrow*! I just need to make sure she is fine. I *swear*! *Please!* If she isn't here tomorrow, I promise you can kick my lyin'-"

"She *betta* be fine," she seethed nothing but venom. Viper sucked her teeth, "Try me, a'ight?" She yelled louder, "Vera, girl, you be a'ight, okay? I'mma be back here to-mor-*row*." She lowered her voice to Derrick, Vera could barely hear, "Life on contract, y'hear? See y'all tomorrow."

Derrick called after Viper, "I went to med school, she's in good hands!"

Vera's blood ran cold. He thinks she's a wondrous medical oddity. Brilliant.

Ideas of running away flashed across Vera's mind but reality struck her – where would she run to? And looking the way she did? Police would pick her up in no time and she *definitely* did not want that.

The farewell song repeated itself three or four times as Derrick closed the store, a slow, melodic cabaret number. Vera tried to calm herself to the music but her nerves kept buzzing. The music stopped and the window covers clanked down. Vera jumped from the harsh bang. She huddled up, unsure what to do.

Derrick breezed into the storeroom, the bright shop lights painted the walls. Vera tried to relax herself, look less like a terrified child, but had little success. She bundled up again when Derrick plopped down cross legged in front of the cot.

"Storytime," he clapped. "Time to tell me *everything*. Let's go."

Vera frowned, "Can't I tell you tomorrow?" It dawned on her how stupid that sounded. This was assuming she still had a job – and wasn't strapped to a medical bed.

Derrick's face fell flat. "Unless you're gonna have a

pretty pie graph, bar charts and a beautiful presentation, I strongly doubt it." Again, he clapped, "Storytime, now."

In vain effort to change the subject, Vera asked, "You went to med school?"

Derrick laughed, "More like 'dropped out'. I got a degree in music. Med school was *way* too hard. So, if you ever have a heart attack, all I know is how to tell you 'you're having a heart attack' and explain how it works as you die. And maybe I'll remember to dial 911. Either way," he clapped, "Storytime. Stop trying to change the subject. How did you grow that gold hairpiece out your head as you slept? I saw it. You were laying there the whole time. Just come *out* with it–"

"I can dream!" Vera blurted.

Derrick's face fell flat again. He cocked an eyebrow, beyond bemused. He blandly remarked, "*That's* obvious. But what about the–"

"It's just ... I can make my dreams come to life ... kinda. It's really hard to explain." Vera took a defeated breath and tried the best she could, "You know how you just saw stuff grow on me?"

"Yeeeeeaaaaaah?" Derrick replied.

"In my dream ... I'm dreaming like anyone else but anything that happens to me in my dream, I wake up with."

Derrick desperately tried to follow, "So ... in your dream ..."

"So, in my dream, I had some pine needles, I think, fall in my hair and it turned into this hairpiece. I was sliding down a hill so that's why I'm dirty ...," Vera trailed off. Out loud, she was certain she sounded completely mad. She wondered if Derrick would be nice enough to lock her away in a nice medical ward. Maybe a room with a view and physicians that will at least ask first before they cut her apart. This wasn't normal and she knew it. Vera shrugged and murmured in shame, "It's somethin' I do."

Derrick still couldn't comprehend. "How long have you had dreams like this?"

Vera gazed away to think for a moment, "Um ... since I was little?"

"Does your mom know?" He questioned. He pushed away what he couldn't understand and tried to focus on the important.

Vera grew more flustered from all the questions, "It's... it ... aw, man–"

"You've been hiding it all this time?" Derrick was astonished.

"No!" Vera squeaked. She blurted, "It runs in the family!" Vera calmed herself to a rational pace, "It's kinda like a gene. A rare gene."

"A gene?" Derrick couldn't believe what he was hearing. "A gene that makes your dreams come alive."

Silence filled the air. Vera reluctantly nodded.

"Anyone else know? Besides ... family," Derrick winced a little on the last part, he knew family was a thorny subject for Vera. He could commiserate, even his cousin today was busting his chops about when he would become respectable: get rid of the tattoos, obtain a decent haircut, go back to med school, little improvements like that. Maybe overhaul the store for classical customers only, something the elders wouldn't balk at. And bring home someone decent – preferably female.

Vera shook her head, "Nope, just you."

"Wow," Derrick uttered in quiet amazement. "You were *far* better in school than me." He snickered, "I slept *too* much in class."

Vera tried to crack a smile but the truth of her being weighed far too heavy.

"Hey, hey," Derrick patted Vera. "You got my word, Vera. I won't tell anyone."

Vera bundled up. She wished none of this ever happened. That this whole day never occurred.

Derrick could see the worry and regret painted on her face. He slapped his thighs, "Let's get you home – Hey, do you mind if I talk to your mom about this? Just to let her know you're fine." He beamed a warm smile.

Vera pondered on it, she knew her mother wouldn't be too happy but she had no other better ideas. "She doesn't get off work for another three hours."

"Hm," Derrick mulled over a plan. After a minute of silence, he snapped his fingers, "I got it! I'll drop you off and just swing by later when your mom gets off work. How about it?"

Vera offered a limp shrug, "I gues–"

"Vera, it's better when everyone in the know is in the know about each *other*. What if you snap your leg in a skiing dream or something?"

She shivered at the thought. "Oh geez." Vera relinquished with a tired wave, "Fine, fine. You got a deal."

Derrick nodded, "Great, let's head out. Give me a few minutes to collect the money and straighten up and we'll be gone."

The duties were quick, he already had done most of the work after the last customer filed out. All that remained was to collect the till, notify cancelled patrons with the option of a reschedule or refund, and that was it. While Derrick blurred through closing, Vera texted her mother.

>   **Vera:** Ma, I'll be home early
>   Derrick is coming by later
>   He saw me.
>   **Vera:** He saw me do the thing
>   Will explain later, plz dun freak out
>   Plz ♥♥♥

Vera powered off her phone. She didn't want to see the reply she'd soon receive. All she wanted to do was go home, curl up small in her bed and never wake up. She couldn't fight the feeling of dread that raked through her.

Derrick sauntered back into the storeroom and clicked off all the lights. "Ready to rock and roll?"

Vera pocketed her phone and rose from the cot. The solid gold fascinator ticked against the bottom of the shelf as she tried to watch her head. The tap made her straighten up faster; she hoped Derrick didn't hear. "Yup!" she said.

Derrick set the alarm and breezed past Vera, "Let's go."

The ride home was devoid of chatter. Deafening moonbeat filled the air as the truck rumbled to Vera's house. The traffic was a little thicker, thanks to the late lunchtime rush.

Once at Vera's home, Derrick turned the music down as Vera unbuckled. "I'll be around at about six, ok?" he confirmed over the idle rattle of the truck.

Vera nodded and got out. She gave the door a hearty slam and waved to Derrick before she went onto the sidewalk. The neighborhood was nothing spectacular. A tan, cracked street lined with few cars and plain, small houses. The Florence house stood out most by its mismatched gate.

Derrick returned the wave and puttered off, moonbeat returning at full blast as he turned the corner.

Vera dug out her keys and opened the gate. The day was pleasant, the wind was brisk. A lovely day but Vera couldn't see past the dark cloud hanging over her head. The colorful spikes in the yard lined her path, soaking up the sun. A couple were tilted and one had a broken cuff.

Vera turned her phone on as she reached the door. A text message from her mother popped up. Vera turned the phone back off and went inside. She threw the front door closed and thumped up the stairs straight to her room.

She slid out her boots as soon as she crossed the

threshold of her room and flopped onto her bed. Dirt and brambles lined the inside of her shoes. Flakes flickered from her stained socks. She groaned when she heard hard bits scatter to the floor. The fascinator had given up a fight when she tried to pry it from her hair. There was no normal attachment, only micro-holes for every strand of hair. More soot tinkered from her socks as she pulled and teased the fascinator out. In a few frustrating minutes, she finally had parted the fascinator from her fluffy hair. It reflected a brilliant gleam, every speck and point captured in beautiful gold. Enrapturing as it was, Vera slid it aside – something new to add to her dream pile later.

The grime that clung to her unsettled her so. She got up and undressed to take a quick shower. Dried mud stained her legs almost to her knees, and her arms still bore crackles of dirt. She fetched a new pair of undergarments from her dresser and hustled to the bathroom.

Her dreams weren't always so adventurous. Sometimes, she had soft, wonderful dreams filled with delight and imagination. Other times, she flew and had daring experiences. Through her dreams, Vera traveled to distant, absurd worlds and embodied all that she wasn't in the waking world. She even found a sincere love that cared for her deeply.

Vera returned to her room wrapped in a towel over her undergarments. Water trickled down her shins as she checked her sopping hair. She hoped she plucked out every hidden pine needle lodged in her tresses.

She rummaged through her clothes pile and pulled out an oversized band shirt. Vera slid it on over her towel and pulled the towel out from underneath. As she clumped the towel up to pat down her legs, it astonished her how milky brown the draining water became when she scrubbed them. Vera checked the towel, no sneaky dirt to be found. She folded the towel up and draped it over her iron headrest.

Vera curled up on her bed in front of the sleeping laptop. With a light tap on the mouse pad, it basked to life and displayed a paused episode of *Mystery Pop Pop*. Vera went back to the episode list, picked the season finale and started watching.

※

The season finale of *Mystery Pop Pop* was as every bit thrilling as Vera had hoped. Though the leaks took some punch out of the twists and turns, the rumors were proven half untrue – Leilani remained on the show, safe and unscathed. The only character that died was Jeremy, the team lackey no one liked. Daymond stepped up from major supporting character to main, co-leading with Leilani. Vera liked the change; his piercing wit matched well with her cleverness and together they became an unstoppable duo, ready for the next season.

Vera still had two hours to blow, so she looked for movies online to watch. Never one to pay for what she could comb out for free, Vera perused her usual digital haunts for free, possibly pirated movies. Wading through the expansive library, she looked for anything light and long. No matter how far and wide she scrolled, nothing piqued her interest. Indecisive, Vera clicked the "Surprise Me" button to the left of the search bar. She was willing to settle with anything, as long as it wasn't too far outside her tastes.

The screen took a moment to refresh with the results. The poster for a campy-looking horror movie called "Mass Graves" appeared. The entire poster was pitch black, and the title dripped with blood and mud. Under the title, a bloody, gloved hand wrapped around the hilt of a dripping butcher knife. In the reflection of the knife, there was a terrified cheerleader trying to crawl away. Beside the poster read a quick synopsis: "Deranged and dispersed from the KGB, former agent hunts unsuspecting campers in forest for a quick thrill. No one can escape The Hunter."

Vera never really cared much for horror but she saw enough of them to know they amused her with their ridiculous effects and terrible clichés. As far as she was concerned, horror movies were merely bloody, backward comedies. To top it all off, it was an hour and a half, too – all the better.

She clicked "play" and began to watch.

※

The movie turned out scarier than originally anticipated. Foreign made, the movie followed none of the tropes Vera expected. It was clear the movie was filmed on a shoestring budget but they made every coin count. Except for the beginning, every scene gushed with blood and terror. The Hunter loved torture and loved it dearly. Calculating. Cold. Blood-thirsty. It wasn't enough for him to simply kill his victims, he had to stalk them down, one by one. He would leave the forest time and time again to drag back more prey. His victims were varied, as were their capabilities. Nary a ditz, dunce, or bimbo in sight. Every victim held a deft skill in something. And The Hunter loved them all, what relishing challenge and joy they all brought him. He could outwit the smartest, overpower the strongest, beguile the cleverest. But he loved the ones that fought back the *most*, they would always make him cackle with a wretched, chilling smile. No one had a clean death, everyone died in stupendous, horrific ways.

The movie ended with The Hunter stalking over a burning hill in the broad daylight. His eyes were a dull blue, his nose slender and his hair a short brown crop. He wore a white leisure suit with a tan turtleneck. Not a speck of blood or dirt on him but his blade was washed red. With all his victims dead, the film faded to black. Stark words bled onto the screen:

> Watch Things Come To An End -
> The Hunter shall become The Hunted
> Mass Graves 2

The words faded away to a dual poster. The original poster appeared on the left, the killer holding a dripping blade bearing the reflection of a terrified victim. On the right was the same design but a ruby manicured hand held the knife and The Hunter cowered in gripping terror in the reflection.

Vera exited out of the screen and wiped her eyes. It was still daytime, so she figured she wouldn't be that affected. This wasn't her first horror film, she had rules: always watch during the day, watch something cute or funny before going to sleep and never watch scary films at night. She checked the clock, there was just enough time to get dressed, greet her mother and expect her boss. Her stomach panged, she wanted nothing more than to zip past this moment.

Vera pushed her laptop off to the side and swung her legs over the side of the bed. She reached over and pulled a pair of black, baggy cargo pants out of the clothes pile. Delicate decorative chains linked between the front and back pockets clinked and clattered as she rested the jeans onto her lap and flapped them out. Vera slid them on and fluffed out her shirt. Digging through her pockets, Vera found a stretched-out hair band to bundle her moist hair with. Flecks of water shook onto her shoulders as she wrapped the band around three times.

Vera took a good look at herself with the long mirror behind her bedroom door, her bare feet poked out from the sop of fabric bundled on the ground. The midnight black of her clothes hid the wrinkles and lint. Her shirt had no stains and though her hair didn't look spectacular, it wasn't a tragedy, either. Vera swung back open the door and crouched down to search for her fuzzy, ocean blue slippers under her bed. Scattered among the rest of her shoes, they were easy to find – it was the only pair she owned with any pop of bright, vivacious color and not chunky or gothic.

Slipping on the slippers, Vera picked up her phone and turned it on. She expected a volcano of excoriating messages as she watched the phone glow and beep to life. Instead, there were only two, the one Vera originally ignored and a new one from twenty minutes ago, both from her mother.

Ma: Ok baby
Ma: On my way

Vera blew out an anxious sigh. Worry crackled in the pit of her chest. But she had to face what was to come. She couldn't help but feel it was the beginning of the end.

※

Adelia was almost home, just a few more minutes left on her boring, usual drive. Light blues wafted from her radio as she took the side streets to avoid traffic. Another mind-numbing day at the office, just like every other day Adelia had worked at shipping logistics company HermesQuik since Vera was born and rose up the ranks from Dispatcher to Dispatcher Manager to Head Supervisor. It was drab and unstimulating, all she did everyday was ensure everyone was on task and steer back the ones that weren't. Sitting on the edge of town, the only perk the job had was the serene drive through the winding, forest roads before hitting coarse cityscape.

At work, Adelia rarely socialized with her co-workers. It wasn't that she didn't like them, she just never felt like bonding with them. Especially the young dispatchers, who would come and go like leaves. They saw no point in throwing down roots. It wasn't their fault, the job was inane and opportunities to move up shrank drastically over the years. She couldn't blame them, she always wanted to leave herself. Perhaps once Vera was out on her own and stable. Maybe a new career in renovation. She always loved working with her hands.

When Adelia got the texts from Vera, disappointment and anger flashed within her. Then concern soaked in, who knows where Vera's dream travelling had sent her to. Adelia remembered when she dream traveled herself as a young girl. Her mother, Aveline, found her floating above the bed one morning. The memories and the ache in her hip flooded back. How her mother screamed and yanked her out the air to the floor by her ankle out of sheer terror. Aveline couldn't stop screaming about possession. Adelia couldn't make heads or tails of her frantic mother. All she knew was that she was in the middle of a flying dream, and then ripped to the floor by her wailing mother. Aveline couldn't contain her distress, she called her mother Victoria and hailed her over quickly. When Victoria came and looked Adelia over as Aveline rambled on about what she saw, Victoria spotted the trait immediately. It was the same as her own sister, Addie, and her mother, Delores. The trait skipped Aveline completely but that never mattered to her, she considered it "devil's work" all the same. And now her daughter, Adelia, had it.

Adelia soaked in everything she learned from grandmother Victoria and aunt Addie. She used to try to thumb through Addie's dream journal but her handwriting was none too legible; she barely knew how to write unless she was tracing the Bible for Sunday sermons. But the stories Victoria and Addie told were more than enough. Then Victoria passed away, and then Addie a couple years later. Since Addie had no children of her own, responsibilities fell down to Aveline, the eldest of the next generation, to bury her.

Aveline stopped at nothing to make sure Addie's dream journal was buried with her. She blustered and snapped at anyone who dared stood in her way. Aveline was sure the journal held the "curse" and that this was the only way to make things right. At least, to fix her daughter Adelia.

To this very day, Adelia never told her mother Vera had the trait and that it existed stronger than it did in Victoria and Addie. Possibly as strong as the ancestors in their stories, if not beyond that. Her mother would probably sink back into hysterics but Adelia knew Addie and Victoria would have been proud to know that only remaining testament of the survival of their bloodline through the heinous toil, maddening terror and infinite torture had survived once more.

But for now, Adelia just didn't want to make the same mistakes her mother made. She never forgave her mother for her belligerence, being thrown to the floor. The roaring lectures, the cups of holy water she was forced to drink, the scriptures scrawled around the walls and all over her bed. She didn't want Vera to know the same, the unrelenting anger. The isolating hatred.

Adelia parked the car in front of the house. It was a well-cared-for oldie, and still ran like new despite being a decade old. She locked the car with a beep and made her way inside. She found Vera sitting on the couch, fearful eyes planted on her. Vera's glowing phone illuminated her chin as it rested on her lap.

Once the door closed, Vera bolted up to her mother, "Ma, I didn't mean to get found out! I–"

Adelia paused her with a sharply raised hand, her eyes closed and brows knitted. She didn't want to hear any more; the anger flared back within her. She pointed to the couch. Vera sat back down silently. Adelia pinched the bridge of her nose. She simply did not know where to begin. She lanced her daughter with burning eyes and wound slow into an angered pitch, "Vera, how did this *happen*? Why were you sleeping at *work*?"

Vera, shifted to the edge of her seat and barreled out, "Ma, we can nap on breaks! I was on break!" She slowed down, the embarrassment slinking in, "Derrick ... my boss found me. I grew a fascinator in my hair and ... and looked like I was dragged through dirt. He ... he saw all of it." Vera hung her head low, "All of it."

Adelia pursed her lips. She couldn't believe Vera could be so daft to commit such a job-costing move but sympathy bled through. A disappointed sigh flared from her nose.

Vera continued, fumbling a chain link on her pants, "He's coming by soon. I was just texting him as you came in." Checking her phone, Vera said, "He's about ten minutes away. He wants to talk about ... about what he saw."

Adelia narrowed her eyes and lifted her chin with suspicion. "Talk about it *how?*" She hardly knew Derrick, she had only met him a small handful of times during the occasions she picked Vera up. He seemed okay but that didn't automatically make him trustworthy.

Her daughter shrugged hopelessly, "I dunno. He just wants to let you know that he knows, I guess."

Adelia pulled in her lips in thought, "Hmmmm." A soft rumble emanated outside, growing louder with a low thumping bass.

Vera's phone belted out a rapid, harsh guitar chord and lit up. It was a new text message.

On the screen, a message from Derrick popped up in a lavender bubble:

Derrick: I'm Outside. Mom home?

Vera craned her head towards the window, she spotted Derrick looking over his shoulder as he parked the truck behind Adelia's maple brown sedan.

"That would be him," Vera pointed. The rumble died and there was a thunderous slam of steel. She typed to Derrick:

Vera: She's home.

Adelia opened the front door and looked through the storm door. Derrick strolled down the stone path with a bright smile and a red tatted arm thrown up in warm salute. He had on a Bauhaus shirt and dark, canvas pants with heavy, black boots. His hair was combed with a clean, flat part and his beard bore a fresh trim. She held the storm door open for Derrick to clod through. He passed her with a polite smile and curt nod, smelling of pleasant spices. He was half a head taller than Adelia, who was a head taller than Vera. Surveying the living room, he found an uneasy Vera shriveled up on the couch. Adelia closed the front door as the storm door swung itself shut.

"Hey, Vera," greeted Derrick. He started to kick off his boots by the door but Adelia tried to stop him, baffled by his actions. Derrick paused for a moment with a blank stare until he noticed what he was doing. With an easy laugh, he explained, "Asian households. We usually take our shoes off at the door. Should I keep them on?"

Seeing his shoes were mostly off, Adelia brushed away the issue, "You're fine, you're fine." She straightened up and politely directed Derrick to the couch.

His boots were off but still his footsteps were heavy and loud. His socks were banker gray and fresh, Vera could tell this was his best impression of "mature, boss adult" that he could muster. He sat beside her, and she bobbed like a lighthouse buoy in the sea when his seat rippled hers. He wasted no time to complement Vera to Adelia, "Vera's an amazing employee. Awesome at *everything*." He leaned back on the couch and draped an arm over the back of it, full at ease. "She's my second brain, Ms. Florence."

Vera tried to crack a smile as she kept her eyes glued to her knees.

Adelia accepted the compliment gracefully. "Thank you, Mr ... uh ... what is your last name? I don't think I ever heard it."

"Ma," Derrick answered confidently, "My last name is 'Ma'."

"Thank you, Mr. Ma," Adelia tried again. "Vera told me you're here because she did something at work? Is everything okay?" She kept her tone light and courteous.

Derrick leaned forward and propped his forearms on his legs. He glanced at Vera for a moment before he said, "Your daughter was napping on break," he rushed out to save "– and that's *fine*! Retail is hard work and she's a hard worker, naps on break time are cool in my book. But Vera... has an *unusual* sleeping habit, I found." Vera shifted uneasily as Derrick continued, "Her dreams come alive and affect her in the real world. She told me you knew she could do this and had never shown anyone else so I just wanted to touch bases."

Shoulders still squared, Adelia held her graceful composure at the news. Vera grounded into the couch with hot anxiety and molted with sheer humiliation.

Adelia responded, "Ah, yes. It's called 'Dream Traveling'. It runs in the family but Vera has a very strong version of it. I hope it didn't scare you."

Derrick blew out a laugh as he shook his head and waved off the thought, "Oh no, no, no. Not at all. I was confused but never scared." He snorted, "It takes a *lot* to scare me. I just had no clue what was happening to Vera."

Adelia turned her eyes to her silent daughter and said, "Vera, you've been quiet this whole time."

Vera's face crumpled up with discomfort. Her voice was soft, she barely had any voice. "Can I go upstairs? I just ... I don't really know *what* to say."

Derrick tittered out a light laugh before Adelia could make Vera repeat herself louder, "You're fine, Vera. Ms. Florence, is there anything I need to know?"

Adelia shrugged, "Nope. But thank you for telling me, Mr. Ma." She added, showing any hint of uncertainty for the first time, "I – I have to admit, this is a little strange. I've never encountered this before. It's been a closely guarded secret in the family until now."

"It still is," Derrick calmly assured. He stood up and reached out a hand for Adelia to shake.

Adelia stepped forward and shook it firmly. Vera kept her eyes down, reading the shadows on the floor.

Derrick gave a light clap, "Let me know if there is anything I can do." He spoke to Vera, "I'll be seeing *you* bright and early. Get a good night sleep, okay?"

Vera bristled at the slight jab. Adelia warmly smiled as Derrick walked over to slide back on his shoes. He opened the front door and showed himself out. Adelia closed the door after him as he clodded down the stone path.

Silence filled the room. Adelia stared at Vera. Vera stared at her knees.

"Veronica," Adelia chided.

Vera sputtered out, "I'm sorry, okay? I messed up and–"

"*Veronica*," Adelia silenced her daughter. She had a stern look in her eyes and sharp edge to her tone. "You are *very* lucky this is all that happened. He may be fine with naps at work but I'm *not*. No more, okay?"

Vera whispered, "Okay." She didn't want to look at her mother. She already knew the look she had carved on her face: anger and disappointment. What else would there be to expect?

Adelia softened her demeanor and walked over to her daughter to sit beside her. She sighed, "Vera, baby, someone finding out is new for me, too."

Vera looked up, "Didn't Dad know?"

Adelia jerked at the mention, "Uh ... your father and I... he – he never knew. We weren't together that long." Vera's father was always a complicated subject. He left when Vera was months old out of stress from being thrown into parenthood so soon at such a young age and in such a new relationship. They only lasted about a little over a year. She grasped Vera's hand and said, "Baby, your dad ... he was a complicated man. He didn't know. Most people ... don't. Maybe back when our family was broken up during bondage and desperately wanted to get back together, everybody knew but now, no." Adelia looked away, "I wish I could tell your father." She looked back at Vera, adding pitifully, "But he was too caught up in himself." Adelia kissed Vera on the temple and changed the subject, "You want pizza for dinner?"

Vera nodded. Her father was a rare subject because he left her mother broken-hearted. It was no secret Adelia wished he stayed. Vera noticed her mother never dated anyone else, just focused on work and renovations. Vera herself had no personal memories of him but sometimes the imagined version of him would appear in her dreams. Together, they would play, have tea parties and snuggle together. One day, Vera wanted to find him but all she had for now was his name: Alvin Camdor. Her mother wouldn't tell her much else out of depression.

Together on Vera's phone, they started looking at what was available, cheap and close.

※

That night, Vera slept soundly in her bed. All the kitten videos she played lulled her to sleep. She dreamt of being at a beautiful ball deep in the lounge of a magnificent ship. The décor was ornate. Crystal chandeliers swayed, and the night sky glittered through the port windows. The grand stairwell rippled down with a flowing red carpet, secured by crystal spiked rods. The steps were deep curved crescents made of the finest woods, just like the rest of the ballroom. Glasses tinkered and clinked arrhythmically. The ball goers chattered about, a few lavished over the tinkering glass. They said it was the best, vivacious piano music they ever heard.

Vera watched the ball from the top of the grand stairs. All the ball goers were beautiful, coiffed and Black. Dressed as if attending a royal ball during the Harlem Renaissance, there were ornate gowns, sparkling flapper dresses, brilliant suits and startling tuxedos. Everyone danced in pairs, frozen but rotating like figures in a music box. The dancers never moved to the next spot themselves, instead they appeared in the next place, switching places as they spun jauntily. Again and again, they swayed and disappeared into the next place.

Vera herself wore a buoyant and bulbous Edwardian ball gown. Strings of pearls curved over the top of her bodice, flower lace covered the front. She pulled a saffron orange tablecloth and draped it over herself. Her dress became a twice fuller ball gown in saffron with a red organza split flowing out. She smeared cake frosting over her arms, they became ivory gloves. Her hair zipped into tight curled braids that ringed about her face and pulled the rest into a pearl and diamond speckled bun. She took a step down the stairs but sailed to the bottom as if by a current of air. The dancers moved around her, some adopting more complicated jitterbug movements as they spun. A couple duos started to slide across the floor as if steered by an invisible base.

A lone dancer touched Vera's waist from behind. A handsome man with deep mahogany skin, long violet dreads pulled back with a golden cuff and a spread of galaxies for eyes. He had a firm, chiseled face with a soft smile and kind eyes. He dressed in a dapper midnight blue tuxedo. Vera whirled around, and a smile bloomed across her face. It was Love, her dream embodiment of all that she wanted and adored. He always filled her with enchantment. Once, Love gifted Vera a glittering jet necklace. She used to wear it everyday until it was nearly stolen. Now, it lived in a special jewelry box atop her dresser.

Love offered a gloved hand with a subtle smile; he wanted to dance. Vera accepted graciously. Love curled an arm behind her waist and off they went onto the gilded dancefloor.

Together they waltzed between the other pairs. The music changed to a muddled yet moving violin concerto. Vera laid her head upon Love's shoulder. Love laid his atop hers. The world was bliss. Then Vera kicked up ice water.

When she looked down, her swirling skirt had a dark hem and the water was already ankle deep. A small cluster of ice skirted into her elegant boot, making her jump. The sting of cold prickled up her spine but Love did not mind, he just tried to lay Vera's head back on his sturdy shoulder. The dancers around them didn't care about the water, either. They would cut the water with brilliant splashes as they spun and kicked.

Love dipped Vera low, and an ice floe brushed past her back. The sudden chill erupted Vera out of the dip and away from Love's arms. Love's face still bore a calm, pleasant look as he simply grasped her hand to continue their dance. He swept her away with a royal turn, water swirling around her ball gown. Vera tried to tap his shoulder and point out the water but he was unfazed.

The roof of the grand ballroom started to raise as if neatly sliced away, and the stars above began to drip in like tumbling fireworks. Vera patted Love's shoulder again and pointed up. Love looked up and smiled at the falling stars. He turned his smile to Vera and kissed her forehead.

"No! No!" Vera said. She had no voice. Vera tried to continue, "We have to go!" Vera pulled out his grasp and tried to tug him along by his wrists but Love wanted to keep dancing.

Some of the falling stars sparked fires wherever they landed. The dancers didn't care, even when the stars would flash them from existence. One nearly landed on Vera but Love swirled her out of the way in time.

Vera agonized but was still mute, "Lovey, *plea–*"

She was snatched through the ground by a hand gripped on her ankle. Vera thumped back on the forest sliding path from her last dream. Except there wasn't a cliff, only a deep expanse of maple and oak trees leaning heavy down a steep decline. The world whizzed by as she slid on her back. The rough earth pulled the bell of her gown over her head. The only thing protecting her legs were her knee-length bloomers. Vera tried to grab for something, anything but her dress extended far beyond her grasp. Flutters of orange and red blinded her, only a small, fluttering gap at the end of her skirt gave her any view as she rolled onto her stomach.

In the distance sliding behind her was a thin, pallid man with a tan turtleneck under a cream leisure suit. He had a thin, razor nose, mousey brown cropped hair and chilling, vicious cold blue eyes piercing her with a steady stare. The Hunter.

Vera could barely see him through the tattering window of her skirt but her heart panged at the sight. The Hunter slid down the slope behind her, focused on his prey. To ping himself faster, he tapped from tree to tree with expert precision. The distance quickly shrank between them. The more horizontal the trees became, the faster The Hunter pinged between them.

Fear gripping her heart, Vera tried to roll onto her back and rise up but she tumbled over herself in a wild plummet down the hill until she slammed into the bottom of a deep grave. Her head struck the ground, and her vision flashed white for a moment. The cleanly dug walls were nine feet tall, the sky was so far away. Her dress was shredded, and she was covered in scratches. A quiet ring pierced her ears.

The Hunter peered over the mouth of the grave, a crazed smile stretched across his face. He craned his head side to side like a deranged owl as he tried to get a better look at Vera. She winced and struggled under her drowning pain. The grave was tight; she couldn't escape his haunting stare. She could barely keep her eyes open.

"Aww, sleepy already?" The Hunter cooed in a heavy Russian accent.

Ice water thundered through the sides of the grave, shocking Vera to her feet. She tried to scramble up the flooding walls but all she could do was grab sopping clumps of mud. Her shoes squished down in the freezing mud, the cold soaked her through and through. She rasped out screams of terror and protest, searching for a grip somewhere, anywhere as chilling water poured down upon her clambering, numb arms. Water filled the grave fast, almost reaching her thighs. With a panicked leap, Vera sprang wall to wall towards freedom. Her body felt light, some of the pain had dissipated.

Furious, The Hunter pulled a cudgel from behind him and whumped it down in rage, catching Vera right down the middle.

"NO CHEATING!" The Hunter screeched. His accent temporarily disappeared. "You're supposed to be DEAD!"

Vera slammed back into the icy waters below with a great splash. Her dress blossomed under the water. Her bodice weighed her down and the skirt slurred her kicks. She had no shoes left; ice prickled her feet. Vera fought to stand upright but the churning waters battered against her. Her lungs prickled and burned from the air she held. She needed to breathe again. Vera broke the surface with a scathing breath.

The Hunter taunted in his returned accent, "Oh! Little girl still wants to play!" He jumped down into the grave with her. The Hunter remained dry in the chest-deep water as he walked smoothly to her.

Vera pressed herself against the pouring wall, terrified. The ice shards embedded in the streams stung her shoulders and arms. They felt like death by a thousand cuts. The Hunter pulled out his long, butcher knife. A reflection of Vera, cornered and afraid, gleamed in the silver of the blade. His thin lips curled into a wiry, demented smile. He lunged at her –

Vera woke up, soaked and pained in her bed. Her ribs jabbed with blaring agony. Every breath she took was a vicious stab. She tried to hold her breath to soothe the stabs but a different agony would replace them, forcing her to breathe again. Her sinuses burned like firecrackers. Every cough felt like a heavy punch. Her ears rang and her head throbbed from concussion. Cuts and sprawling bruises covered her body. Her face was contorted and soaked, covered with splatters of mud. Her ballroom hair had lost all its glitter, it laid disheveled and dirtied as it held the cold to her scalp. Vera blinked and tried to take in her surroundings. She was in her room, in her bed, away from the forest. She attempted to move her leg, but the pain winced her eyes shut and she creaked out a muted yelp. Vera grew still, she couldn't tell if she had cracked ribs. She hoped she didn't.

Nightmares were not new to Vera but this was the first one since she was eight that tried to kill her so ruthlessly.

Tears trailed down her face. Her throat was too raw to call for her mother. She coughed again, spots of mud among her spittle. Vera gathered what tattered will she had left and carefully slipped a leg to the floor. Drilled with pain but nothing broken so far. Her dress was gone, only her sleep shirt remained, an oversized band shirt. Vera sucked in a bracing breath and sifted the rest of herself out of bed, gingerly and slow.

Vera sloshed onto the floor in a crumpled heap; her legs could not stand. She cried in silence from the crushing agony that soaked through her. When she clung to the side of her bed to pull herself up, flashbacks of The Hunter surged to her. Vera froze. Even in the movie, he wasn't this brutal. She tried to remind herself that she was home and awake. She continued pulling herself up, her shoulder burning.

She collapsed onto the floor from the pain.

❦

Vera found herself in another dream. She was horrified, laid out on the warm ground. She wanted to wake up. The world around her was a wide, snowy plain. A beautiful crystal blue sky hung above. The chill of the snow bled into her, numbing her pain. Vera looked about but couldn't lift her head. Around her, snow started to bloom into a serene meadow of wildflowers.

Tree leaves sprouted beside her skin and laid upon her, becoming moss. The moss fanned across her body, digging shallow roots into her. Panic bled into her until she felt the pain and numbness ebb away. The moss shifted red in floods, drawing away her agony. Once they turned their brightest, the moss died and disappeared in patches.

Cleared of all the moss, Vera sat up. She felt new and healthy again. Her head was clear, and there was nary a nick on her skin. She could draw breath and speak unfettered. Perfect and whole. Beneath her, the ground turned into brown school tiles. Paper cut-outs of desks and walls folded up around her. Her breath started to quicken.

"What time is it! Check the time!" She shouted out. "What time is it? Check the time!" She found herself in a narrow desk aisle. The sky became a school ceiling that started to drift down.

Around the fifth yell, Vera darted open her eyes. Early morning basked through her window. She wondered how long she was out as she propped herself up from the floor, healed and dry. Her braids were fuzzy, her bun smashed and the ringlets were stretched and wonky. Vera stood up and checked her phone: 5:21 AM.

Vera dreaded the idea of going back to sleep. Besides, her bed was soaked. Streaks of blood and dirt marked where she laid. Memories of her water grave flashed back to her and her heart raced. She reminded herself that she was awake and healed with a firm shake of her head. She picked up her laptop and when she felt the damp underside, Vera sat back down on the floor and decided to re-watch the first season of *Mystery Pop Pop* until her phone alarm rings.

Chapter III

Vera arrived at work a half hour earlier than usual. She headed out after the second episode of *Mystery Pop Pop*, she didn't bother to wait for the alarm. She tried to change her sheets but the damp made everything a clingy mess. Besides, her mattress was soaked, she had rather let it dry first. She opened her window a little wider to let in the sunlight and heat and hoped her mattress would be dry by the time she got home. Vera moved at her own pace to shower, dress and leave, she had nothing but time. The free bus pulled up as soon as she stepped onto the stop and the ride was a quiet trip under the hazy morning sun.

With the yellow and brown bus rumbling into the distance, Vera walked across the lot the stubby row of stores shared. Four in total, YinYue shared the middle with the auto parts store Tires, Shocks and More. They were locked up like a fortress; locks all over the steel grate covering the doors and windows, security stickers slapped about haphazardly. On the other side of YinYue was Royal Pizzeria, which had been around forever. A faded and sun-bleached paper taped to the grand window with crackled, yellow tape displayed the hours. One could see the columns of stacked pizza boxes against the wall and over the soda coolers. On the other side of the auto store was Happy Words, a stationary store bedecked with Korean advertisements and cute QR clings for deals and coupons. Derrick always got free markers and paint pens from there, and in exchange, he would sell them instruments and practice time with deep discounts. Oily cross patch gates covered the door and picture window.

Vera strolled around the corner behind Happy Words as she scrolled through her phone. Nothing interesting on Twip or any of her favorite sites. Memories of last night drifted back. Residual pain waved through her body as she tried to will it away with more mindless scrolling. She regretted watching *Mass Graves*.

In a minute's pace, she was at YinYue's loading dock. Long morning shadows crossed over the empty back lot. Vera hoisted herself onto the dock's ledge with a couple tries. She walked to the double doors and fished out her keys. She sorted through them until she found a gunmetal purple key and entered it in the weather-beaten lock. It was stubborn but with a few stern tries, the key turned and she walked open the heavy door outwards. She could hardly open the doors normally, she always walked them open. She waltzed in past the slow sweeping door and heard it bang shut behind her. The lights above her turned on, sensed by the motion detector near the doors. A shrill beep sounded: the alarm system. Vera went to the alarm panel tucked between the door and the dingy motion sensor and tapped in her code on the bright, lime lit keys. The panel accepted with a cold beep.

Vera's boots clicked down the storeroom hall in the morning quiet. She slid her phone into the back pocket of her baggy cargo pants. Her shirt was a deep blue and brandished a faded smiley face with crossed out eyes. She turned on the store lights and entered the shop.

Sunlight filtered through the dirty metal slats. Vera hopped over the triplet of stairs behind the counter and pulled out the thick work gloves. Dingy and tough, the fingers were too stiff for her to be nimble. She could feel nothing, it took three tries to get a solid grip on the thin chain. The slats rose one by one with every terse pull. When she first started, her shoulders used to burn when she raised the gate, now they didn't. She clanked every slat to the very top and tucked the chain back behind the row of decorative record albums. Vera turned around – and was given a start by Derrick, who stood propped against the storeroom doorway. His arms were crossed, a smirk stretched wide across his face as he held a brown, covered cup of convenience store coffee.

"You're such a good worker," he beamed with a morning tone.

Struggling to quell her hammering heart, Vera

snapped, "You *scared* me! Don't *do* that!"

Derrick snickered as he peeled away from the doorjamb. His eyes swept over the store, "How did you sleep last night?"

Vera shook off the gloves with a single flick and threw them back over the aluminum bat as she answered honestly, "Ehhhh, I saw a scary movie before you came and took it to bed with me."

Her boss' face cleared to a look of stupefaction as he stared at Vera while she stood at the shop computer. "Really? I'd figure with your … trait, you'd steer clear of those. I would!" He took a pensive swig of his lukewarm coffee.

Vera shrugged, "Scary movies usually don't scare me." She checked the store's social media accounts. No new messages. A few clicks revealed Derrick had sorted everything out last night. A message in Chinese popped up. There were times mentioned; Vera guessed it was probably a practice room request. She left it unread, Derrick would get to it later.

"But this one did," Derrick noted. He chewed on the rim of his cup.

"I guess," Vera brushed off. She checked the overnight stats, nothing outstanding stood out to her.

Derrick raised an eyebrow and moseyed over to the counter, "*That* was enthusiastic," he balked.

Vera turned to Derrick, "I'm still new to you knowing." She turned back to the computer slowly, "I'm not exactly going to spill every teeny detail of my dreams." She didn't want to remember the torturous agony, let alone share any detail of it. She still wasn't sure if Derrick would turn her over for research and a quick honorary degree if she did. She normally trusted him but what she had was not normal. Vera used to think her mother embellished the stories about grandmother Aveline until the subject of dream traveling was brought up by a cousin a few cookouts ago. Vera had never seen her grandmother so furious and quick to anger. She was usually a calm, reserved, Bible-toting church elder that rarely spoke louder than a sly chuckle.

Derrick threw up his arms. "Hey, hey," he surrendered, "you're cool, I just want to make sure you didn't get dragged through dirt or anything again. I'm not going to play therapist or anything. I probably suck at that."

Befuddled, Vera tossed back, "You hold, like, two group therapy things on Sunday after closing."

Hands still raised, Derrick accepted with a proud smirk and shrug, "Somebody's gotta do it. Besides, I don't suck *as* bad as some of the ones I've been in front of." He dropped his arms and marveled, "Plus, Sunshine Sundays and Happy Sundays have been a *hit*. Speaking of which, check the computer? Which Sunday is it this week?"

Vera pulled up the shop calendar. "ESOL."

Sipping on his coffee, Derrick hummed for a moment before he quipped, "Those have pretty good turnouts, too."

Derrick started the Sunday series about five months

ago. For three Sundays every month, there would be get-togethers an hour and a half long after close. "Sunshine Sundays" were for people, primarily youth and young adults in the Chinese community, to relieve stress, talk about their feelings and get group support over their life problems. "Happy Sundays" were the same but for the queer members of the Chinese community. "ESOL Sundays" were for those who sought to improve their shaky English. The get-togethers were English based but conversations commonly faded in and out of Mandarin, Cantonese and Taiwanese. Vera usually came out of interest but would spend her time straightening up the store so not to intrude. It astonished her to see Derrick so involved with his community. Countless times has she overheard him gripe over his feelings of being an outsider in his own world – sometimes even wishing he wasn't so different. Vera knew how he felt, she just never could see herself doing the same. Open up spaces and invite the same community that never really welcomed her? She couldn't even fathom it.

Vera checked the calendar again, it was Thursday.

"It's international music day," she said. "What we playin' for International Music Hour?"

Derrick paused to think. He then pointed, "Anything but hallyu. I nearly impaled myself with a drumstick last week with that on. Too, *too* many people asked if I was Korean and one White girl called me 'oppa'. *No*." Vera snorted a muffled snicker at the computer as Derrick languished on, "Even my sister who loves that stuff don't do that and I'm actually her *brother*. Not even *jokingly*. Anything but that. Even polka will do." Derrick snapped his fingers, struck with an idea on the tip of his tongue, "Hey, hey, how about that South African one? Spoke-ehhh... Something 'Spoke' ..."

Vera suggested, "Spoek Mathambo?"

Derrick lit up, "Yeaaaaah! That guy! Play him! And slip in some Polysics. It's been a while since I heard from them." He beamed at his own suggestion.

"Okay," said Vera. She opened up the store's music player and started to set up the playlist but she noticed something. "Derrick, Spoek is already in our normal rotation."

His eyebrows jumped up, "He is? ... Ehhh, still international. Play him anyways." It felt good to be king.

"Aye aye, capt'n!" Vera saluted. She placed the artist on the international playlist and selected the morning music. As tingy harpsichord wafted from the store speakers, Vera asked, "Derrick, what's gonna be done about Indie Hour tomorrow? Viper's already gonna be on it but who else?"

Derrick sipped again, mulling over his choices. "Hmmmmmmmmm, The Dowry Effect and Lumination Rising, easy. They both are still indie and just had a tour."

Vera chipped in, "Oh! And Lumination just had a new album out, *Throwing Stones*. Dowry's got one comin' soon, too, but it doesn't have a title yet."

Derrick nodded, "All the more reason."

Adding the two bands to tomorrow's line up for Indie Hour, Vera asked, "Did you hear about the lead singer in

Lumination, though?"

"Ahhhhh, I don't listen to hearsay and talk," Derrick rolled his eyes. "People throw glass in shows all the time. It's called 'getting bottled'. I may or may not have engaged in such practices myself in my youth," he slyly admitted. "It's a good thing the bassist is getting better, though. It must be scary to lose an eye."

"I know, right?" Vera agreed. "Who else is getting added?"

"Ehh, anyone but Rikers, honestly," Derrick said. "Poor production, poor lyrics, hurts my ears. Just no."

Vera chuckled as she made her picks and added them to the playlist. Satisfied with her selection, she came down from behind the counter and the both of them continued opening the store.

※

The day proceeded like all others, dull and quite quiet. A young, pasty-skinned boy tried to slip away with a handful of guitar picks but Derrick tapped him on the shoulder and pried every single pick out the boy's hand. He grabbed the thief by the scruff of his collar and marched him to the front of the store so Vera could take a picture and then threw the kid out. A regular day at YinYue.

Around six o'clock, Viper strolled in. As international music started to play, Viper looked around, coiffed and striking. The free bus was on time today, no need for another long walk in the awful heat. She had on her work shirt, paired with distressed jeans and heeled pastel sneakers. The moment she spotted Vera climb back up behind the counter, she sped to her.

"Vera!" Viper exclaimed as she shifted her shiny black purse to her other arm. "How you doin'? You okay?" She leaned over the counter and felt Vera's forehead with the front and back of her hand. Her nails were bright, long and sharp. A new manicure. Though Viper and Vera were only five years apart, Viper couldn't help but dote on her like a mother.

Vera appreciated the attention, "I'm fine, Viper. I really am."

Viper still eyed Vera for any sign of ill health. "All right. Just wanna make sure you doin' okay. You like my lil' sister, I 'on't want nothin' bad happenin' to you." She scanned the store, it was calm but a little busy. "Where Derrick at?"

"Gettin' some pizza and fries from Royal," Vera answered. "I'mma be heading out soon when he gets back since my shift is over."

"Oh, okay," Viper replied. "You head northeast, right?"

"Nah, south," Vera corrected.

"Ahhh, I see." Viper scanned the store once more, "I'mma hang about. Steer Derrick my way when you see him, ok?"

Vera nodded, "Sure."

Derrick walked through the front door, holding a large box of pizza with a white, greasy bag of fries stapled shut on top. "I'm back, Vera. You're free to go."

"Dibs on the fries," Vera reminded.

Derrick shuffled the box to one hand and grabbed the fries. He readied his throw, "Viper, duck." He chucked the fries underhand over Viper's head. Vera caught the bag with a sound, papery clap.

"I'm gone, y'all," Vera saluted. She closed out her screens on the shop computer. Then she stopped short. "Oh! Derrick! Viper wanna talk to you." Satisfied with herself, she bounded from behind the counter as Derrick walked past.

"Give me fiiiiiiiiive minutes and I'm all yours, Viper." He waved blindly, his back turned, "See you, Vera."

Vera waved back and left, done with another shift. Viper returned the wave as Derrick took the pizza into the storeroom.

❧

Adelia made mac and cheese with bits of ham drizzled in. The home filled with a heavy, heated smell of meat and cheese. Vera stepped through the door just in time, Adelia had turned off the stove and set out the dishes. The kitchen was bright and cozy with red tiled floors, pale cream walls stained with brown flecks of grease, and half curtains hemmed with lace. A bronze legged table sat off to the corner, scuffs under the chairs from the years of wear. The copper, bottom scorched saucepan burbled and steamed with residual heat.

Adelia placed down the last spoon, "Hey, baby, how was work?"

Clutching her empty, balled up paper bag, Vera clodded over to the dining table and plopped into her seat. "Work was alright. I had a bad dream last night, though." She gave the trash can a free throw and sank the shot. She kicked off her shoes as she stretched her shoulders.

Adelia picked up the simmering saucepan and brought it to the table. She picked up her spoon and poured out Vera's serving. "'A bad dream'?" She echoed. "Was it about Mr. Ma coming over?" Adelia scraped the lip of the saucepan and started to fill her own dish.

Vera scrunched her face to one side and shook her head. "I watched somethin' and a dude was in my dream beating me up *bad*." Adelia stopped, she stared as her daughter continued, "I thought he had me for *good*. I was drowning and *everything*."

Adelia dropped everything and scooped up her child, searching for injuries. "My *god*, are you hurt anywhere? Are you okay?"

A bit muffled by her mother's shoulder, Vera replied, "Ma, I'm fine. I had another dream where some moss took the pain away. It was just ...," she trailed off. The memories flooded back, hollow patches of pain returned. "I ... I was *so* terrified. It was so *terrifying*. I thought that dude was gonna kill me for sure." She tried to subdue the water in her tone.

Adelia fluttered kisses over Vera's braided crown. "You're here, baby," she reminded quietly. "You survived.

Did you do the time check trick I taught you for bad dreams?"

"I couldn't think of it at the time," Vera admitted, "but I did it in the other dream when I thought he was coming back."

"Good girl, good girl," Adelia praised.

A tear streamed down Vera's cheek, the water rose in her voice, "I was *so* scared." She whispered painfully, "I don't wanna die in my dreams. I don't wanna die in my sleep."

Adelia's heart panged, she felt helpless. She kissed Vera's crown once more and empathized, "I know, baby. I know." She sat down opposite of her morose daughter and began to eat.

Vera didn't have the stomach to eat past a couple bites. Her tears displaced her hunger. Instead, she left the table to go upstairs. Adelia watched her slink away, head heavy with fatigue and worry.

Worn from her shift and wearied by her tears, Vera decided to head to bed early. She opened her laptop and cued up some animal videos, anything to take her mind off the dreams. As little frolicking kittens mewed and tousled on her screen, Vera changed into her bed clothes and tested her bed. Fairly dry, only damp when pressed deep. Vera took her blanket and burrowed into her bed.

In minutes, she drifted off to sleep.

In her dream, Vera enjoyed standing stage-side of a raucous rock concert. The venue was small and the crowd was packed. The mosh pit swirled with bodies, loud, joyous and rowdy. Lights swept over the crowd from the vibrating speakers, the air shook with every beat and chord. The band was faceless and thrilling, they gave a thundering show. Vera stood among strangers with ripped tees and dangling pants chains. They jumped to the beat or whistled during the solos.

Vera scanned the pit crowd, she discovered Love at the front gate. Still and captivated, Love wore a black band shirt checkered with an imagined logo. The crowd surged around him but he never moved, as if he were the only one standing there. Vera smiled and danced to the pounding melodies. She spun around and stopped.

Off the side of the stage was a metal, dingy ramp leading into a plain office hallway, filled with crisp fluorescent light. Plain and boring, it struck her. Shadow roadies bustled back and forth in the gulf of darkness the ramp crossed over, shuttling about travel crates and wires.

The noise drowned out the solemn footsteps of a man storming forth with pointed determination. He was cloaked in black from his backwards cap to his billowing trench coat, his cold blue eyes pierced from the distance. The Hunter.

Vera jolted awake. Moonlight marked over her room in the cool twilight as Vera heaved for air. The soft gust chilled the sweat on her arms. Her laptop was dark, she tapped it awake and cranked up the brightness. Her eyes burned as it adjusted to the bask. A paused animal video displayed with a message box: "Are you still watching?"

Vera exited the page, her eyes still blurry and squinted, and pulled up *Mystery Pop Pop*'s episode page. She then closed that page and went through her history to pull up the animal video page she just closed. It took a moment for the video to load but soon, little bunnies hopped around as they chased a baby duck around a lakeside. Vera slumped down and tried to watch, anything to soothe her jackhammer heart.

༄༅༅

Work was plain, just like the day before. Nothing spectacular, nothing exciting. A little old lady came in and waxed poetic about vinyl to Derrick for a solid hour and a local battle of the band promoter tried to take over the bulletin board but Vera gave him a quick chat and handed all his flyers back. A regular day.

Viper danced in at the start of Indie Hour, excited to hear her song as the first play. She had asked Derrick yesterday if she was going to get play again and she nearly snapped his neck with joy when he told her she was the kick-off song. Brimming with energy, Viper chatted with Vera at the counter as Derrick overheard, smiling to himself as he managed the new practice room requests. Behind her, Rikers strolled in with his usual bravado.

"Hello, hello, hello, has the world heard my greatness?" said he, arms out wide as he made his way to the counter. He wore fit, ripped jeans and a loose shirt with a shiny gold bracelet.

Viper turned on a sharp heel, a deep cherry sneer carved on her face. Those two never got along.

Derrick zipped from behind the counter, "Rikers, we had this conversation before, there's no *way* I'm playing your stuff in this stor–"

All of Rikers dropped; his face, his arms, his ego. "Maaaan, you *always* do this to me!" He snarled, his gold canines bared, "This why ain't *none* of us gonna get ahead! You sittin' here not playin' nobod–"

"*I'm* gettin' played," Viper interjected. Her voice was calm but simmered with acid. Vera kept an eye on her.

Rikers stared at her, gobsmacked. He pressed his hands together and chided, "Sweetheart, I am talkin' to *him*, not you–"

Viper bucked off the counter, her gold bangles clattering on her raised arm, "Call me 'sweetheart' one more tim–"

Vera reached over and caught Viper's shoulder. Viper backed into the counter as she spat, "Ain't nobody tryna hear yo' bum *lines*, Rikers!"

Store goers started to drift to the front. A couple took out their phones.

Derrick sighed and tried to defuse the storm. "Hey, hey, keep it civil. Rikers, I already said you need to come far better if you want to get on the playlist. Viper's on the list because she earned it–"

"You got a *female* on the list but not me?" Rikers ripped.

Vera could feel Viper bristle under her hand. She held her grip.

Viper shot back, "At least he got a *female* and not a lame bitc–"

"Viper!" Derrick interrupted.

Rikers turned for something to throw, but Derrick clutched his skinny wrists and piled them into a single hand. He yanked Rikers close and seethed, *"Not* in this store." Rikers tried to roar at Derrick but Derrick roared louder, "Knock it off and take a *walk,* Rikers! This is why you can't get on the list! If you can't respect my store or the other people on the list, you can't get on it yourself!"

Vera scanned the store, her grip tight as ever on Viper. Nary a pair of eyes were unfocused on the commotion. Anxiety crackled in her chest, everyone was watching them.

"Rikers!" Vera called out, her voice shaking. *"Please* try to calm down and take a walk!"

Infuriated, Rikers yelled back, "I ain't gon' do *nothin'* you tell me–"

Derrick walked Rikers to the door as he fumed with restrained politeness, "Let's have a nice talk outside, shall we? Vera! Hold down the fort, I'll be right back."

Vera responded, wavered, "Okay!" She felt Viper tug under her shaking hand. She knew better than to let go.

Viper's head followed Rikers' march out the store. Her blood boiled as she watched him with cruel venom in her eyes.

Everyone watched Rikers and Derrick in the middle of the parking lot. The day was overcast and a little breezy. Derrick still kept his iron grip on Rikers' wrists as Rikers unloaded on him. No one could hear anything, just see Derrick's face chiseled with irritated anger as Rikers roared about, trying to jerk himself free.

Then Derrick's face fell flat, Rikers had said something particularly horrid. When Rikers yanked his arms away, Derrick let go, face frozen. Rikers stumbled to the ground from his own momentum. Derrick presented himself openly and dared Rikers to do something. Rikers got up and charged at Derrick but stopped short. Instead, he flipped Derrick off and stormed away. Derrick cupped his mouth and yelled something back. He then turned and went back into the store, bridled with anger.

Parts of the crowd tried to pretend to resume shopping when Derrick came back in. Others stayed still, watching. He saw the crowd and capped his anger. He apologized with a loud clap and shopkeeper's smile, "I am *so* sorry that just happened. Everything is handled, all is solved. Please continue shopping. Thank you for your patronage at YinYue: Music Under the Moon."

A bit more of the crowd dissipated, some still tried to watch. Derrick continued smiling, even as he walked up to Viper. Vera still clutched Viper's shoulder. Viper glowed with hatred.

"Vera, you can let Viper go now," Derrick said, his jaw tight with restraint. Vera unhanded her slowly as he continued talking to Viper in his strained calmness, "I get that Rikers is not your best friend but–"

"He started it!" Viper protested. Vera hovered her hand over Viper's shoulder.

Derrick pressed on with his constrained smile and gritted through his teeth, "But you can't *destroy my store*." He recomposed himself for a second. "I've seen you fight. You're a whirlwind. Not here. Rikers wasn't right but give me a break, okay?"

Viper still steamed but she agreed. "Whateva. But you *need* t' tell Rikers that he keeps talkin' like that–"

"He's not going to be back for a while. He ran his mouth a little too far this time. He gave me some ching-chong nonsense and I told him to take his best shot." Derrick instructed, "Vera, Rikers can't come back here for three months. Got it? You're free to go."

Vera glanced at the clock. It was well past six, almost six-thirty. She looked back at Derrick in concern. She wondered if she should clock in some extra time to give him a moment to cool off.

Derrick read her face. He climbed up behind the counter, "I'm fine. Go home."

༶

When Vera stepped through the front door, her mother was waiting for her on the couch.

"Vera, baby," Adelia started as soon as she saw her daughter, "You want to watch somethin' fun tonight? I found a good movie." She beamed a hopeful smile.

Vera thought about the offer as she closed the door. She felt drained. But she didn't want to go to bed early nor did she want to re-watch any of *Mystery Pop Pop*. Besides, maybe a different, lighter movie will take The Hunter away.

She shrugged, "I s'pose," and flumped down next to her mother. Vera slipped under Adelia's arm and snuggled close. Sleep tugged at her but she stayed awake.

Adelia cued up the movie on the television from her tablet, it began to play. It was an animated feature, filled with silly, bulbous creatures and a claymation sky.

As the opening credits rolled, Adelia asked, "How'd you sleep?"

Vera droned, "Errrgh, I ... he showed up again."

"He did? Did he ..."

"Nah, nah, I woke up before he got near me," Vera answered, focused on the movie. A little, bright lamb clicked about with its chattering hooves across hilly farmland, looking for a moving black hole that was sneakily gliding behind it.

Adelia sighed, "Baby girl, your great grandmother always said these things happen and to try to push through, but ... this is serious."

Vera looked up, "Did great grandma or auntie Addie ever have to deal with this?"

Adelia replied, "That's how they taught me the time trick. Grandmother said it got her out most of the time. Auntie Addie, too. With how the times were back then, I'm certain they had bad dreams. I've had bad dreams, too – everyone does – but yours are tearin' you up so vicious."

"Think grandma ever dream traveled?"

Adelia answered before Vera could finish, "If so, Ma

certainly kept it to herself."

Silence soaked the air. The playful, bumbly creatures danced and sang their woes and joys under a changing, colorful sky. Vera started to nod off but jerked herself awake.

"You okay?" Adelia checked.

Vera rubbed her eyes and tried to focus on the bleary, bright television.

"Maybe you should go to bed," Adelia suggested. "Do you want to sleep in my bed?"

Vera shook her head as she lifted herself to yawn. "I'm good."

Adelia patted Vera's side, "Go to bed, baby."

Vera slumped back over her mother. She was bone tired, rest kept calling her.

"You slept fine out here," reasoned Adelia, "maybe you'll be fine upstairs."

Vera groaned as she raised herself upright. She stood up from the couch and dragged herself upstairs. Her footsteps were slow and deep on the creaky stairs. At her bedroom door, she called downstairs, "Niiiiiiiiight."

"Night, Vera," Adelia called back. She flipped channels until she landed on a sci-fi western that caught her eye.

Vera changed into her night clothes and slipped into bed. She pulled her laptop onto her thighs and pulled up a soft music stream. She picked a nature overlay, something to comfort her. A delicate concerto trickled out over a babbling brook and distant thunder. Satisfied, Vera reduced the brightness to its lowest point and tried to get some rest.

It did not take long for Vera to drop off. In her dream, she fell onto the grey, cold floor of a lonely spotlight. The world was pitch dark around her. She was in her day clothes, the chill of the floor bit her palms and soaked through her pants. A gentle hand cupped her arm and helped her up. Vera looked up with a cherished smile. Icy blue eyes pierced back at her. The blue became flat and the pupils turned chilling white.

Vera yanked her arm away and ran into the darkness, full sprint. The Hunter remained in the spotlight, trailing behind her with a brisk walk. No matter how hard her legs pounded, The Hunter gained ground.

Every time Vera checked over her shoulder, The Hunter was a few feet closer. She felt like she was running through molasses but she saw her legs drill across the floor. Then she tripped and fell down a forest slope. Light dusk covered the forest under a grey sky.

Vera tumbled wildly down the hill. Dirt flew into her mouth, her shoulder cracked against a rock. Her back slammed against the barrel trunk of a diagonal oak tree, it knocked all the wind out of her.

She was filled with sheer pain. Her eyes were fastened shut but she could still see clearly through them. The Hunter tapped from trunk to trunk with a long, silver switchblade in hand. It gleamed and glittered in the fading light. Not a fleck or a speck of dirt or mud stained his cream leisure suit.

Vera moaned in agony, sapped of all strength and will. The Hunter landed with a light tap on the lopsided tree beside her, his crisp white loafers unsoiled by the world around them. His razor thin lips twisted into a broad, toothy smile. He savored this, relished in every minute, every moment.

He hopped a single foot onto Vera's tree and balanced between the two trunks. Vera tried to pull away but she was still winded and pained, draped over the trunk like wet leather. The Hunter scooped up her dangling wrists with a single hand and held them up. He plunged his switchblade deep into her left wrist and slowly pulled it down her forearm. Vera erupted into a maddening scream, as fiery torture burned through her arm. The Hunter smiled wider. She cried louder when he stabbed her again on the other wrist and dragged open flesh. Blood poured over their hands and ran down her arms. The Hunter bathed in her screams like a sweet serenade.

He leaned over and whispered in Vera's ear, "Let's go for a little ride."

The Hunter jumped off both trunks and slid down the forest floor, dragging Vera off the tree and pulling her behind him. The forest ripped at her like a bed of claws as she emptied her lungs again and again, begging The Hunter to stop. Guided by The Hunter's banks and turns, Vera slammed against the rough bark of countless trees while he remained pure and impeccable. Even his sleeves were not washed by her blood.

They slowed to a stop at a leveled part of the path. The

Hunter unhanded Vera and stood up. His hands were clean, his knife gone. He sauntered confident and joyous to her hips, admiring his handiwork. Her body was battered and shredded, her clothes ripped to tatters. The Hunter flashed a wicked smile at Vera's attempt to struggle away as her arms pooled over the groundcover. He knelt down beside her. She was silent, her throat raw and dry. She coughed clotted dirt and debris.

He spoke to her, tender and kind, "Liked the ride? Why, look at you. So sad and breathing." He pulled out behind him his switchblade, clean and gleaming, "Let me fix that. I'll make it all better. I promise, my little bird–"

"Vera, my *god*!" Adelia shrieked, shocking Vera out of the dream.

The room was bright. Blood was everywhere, soaked into the bed and the sides of the pillow. Vera could barely see past the pain but she witnessed her flooding arms laid beside her head. The world seemed so light.

When Adelia ripped back the blanket, she discovered the horror that was her daughter's mangled body. Her sleep shirt was tattered to shreds, her body covered in dirt and blood oozed out everywhere. The sheets under her arms glittered, slick with crimson.

"Please God, *no*! Vera! *Vera*!" she cried out. "My baby, my precious child, *no*!"

Vera coughed, her mouth tasted of blood, dirt and phlegm. She turned her head away and coughed more, her throat and ribs seared and panged. Her pillow squelched lightly under her fits. Too dazed to cry, she stared into nothing.

Adelia raced to the bathroom and yanked down every towel she could see. Stuffed into her arms, Adelia zipped back and tried to staunch the flow.

"Vera? Vera!" Adelia called out to her daughter. She saw her daughter's eyes drift to her languidly. "Vera, baby, *please* stay with me! Stay with me. Don't drift off!" She pressed down hard, a towel on each wrist and the rest piled across her daughter's body. Adelia panicked, "There's too much! Hold on, *please*! Please hold on for mommy. Please, baby!" Adelia piled on more towels and held down harder. She thought Vera's arms would snap from the pressure but she pressed on.

Agony sawed at the light-headed Vera. She wished she could stop breathing, to stop the terrible ache of every drawn breath. Her mother sounded a bit distant and hollow, muddied even. The world seemed unreal, almost dream-like.

Adelia wailed in desperation, "Vera! Vera, please! You don't want this but you *have* to go to the hospital! I will be there, baby. We have to go."

Vera threw her head side to side, rejecting the idea.

"Vera! You're *dying*!" Adelia shrieked.

"Derrick ...," Vera rasped. Her thoughts swam. Her tongue slurred and trailing, she said, "Medic ... call–"

"You want Derrick to take you to the hospital? Baby, it's midnight!" Adelia grew frantic, there was so much blood.

The only sign of life she had of her daughter was her voice and slow blinks.

Adelia feared her daughter was delusional from blood loss. "Baby, he's your boss, not a doctor!" She trailed off into tears, "Baby, please ..."

"Med school ...," Vera mumbled. "Went to ... med school."

"What? Derrick?" Adelia sniffed and re-crumpled the towels for a clean spot. Almost all of the towel was a varying shade of red.

Vera rattled out with an irritated crescendo, "Yes!"

Adelia paused. She never would have guessed Derrick Ma as any sort of doctor but she didn't care, any port in a storm. She searched Vera's room for her phone, discovering it in Vera's pants pocket. Vera's fingers coated with blood, she placed the phone against one of Vera's cleaner fingers to unlock it. Adelia found Derrick in the contacts and called. As the phone rang, she pinched the phone against her shoulder and resumed applying pressure.

Derrick picked up in two rings, "Hello?" He was home, steeping peach tea for himself as his silver cat laid curled up beside the tea box on the counter. His home was small, chaotic and filled with art. He still had on his regular clothes, only his shoes were off.

"It's Vera's mother!" Adelia rushed. "Can you come over, please? She's bleeding out from a dream!"

"What?" He stopped what he was doing.

"She's *dyin'*! A dream she had cut her badly! *Please*!" Adelia begged.

Alarm flared inside him. "I'll be right there, hold on." He hurried to his front door, where a mess of shoes laid.

As he teetered on one foot to put on a boot, Adelia urged, "Get a first aid kit! Hurry!"

"Okay, gotcha." Derrick hung up. He dropped to the ground to get his thick boots on better. His socks were mismatched and splotched with bleach stains.

Adelia placed the phone aside, blood smeared on the side of the case. She kept on her heavy pressure. The towels squished under her weight and there were few discernable clean spots left. Her daughter laid lifeless with shallow breath.

"Vera, baby? You still with me?" Adelia checked. "Try to look at me, okay?"

Vera's eyes drifted to her mother and drifted away.

"Goooooood. Good, baby. Good, Vera," Adelia praised, renewing her pressure. Blood squelched under her hands and beaded between her fingers as she pressed back down. She tried not to break down but tears wouldn't stop rolling down her cheeks.

"Try to hold on, baby," she choked. "Derrick's comin', okay? We're all gonna make you better, okay? Just stay with me. *Please*, baby girl, don't leave me. You're my only pride and joy."

A few more minutes of pressure holding, Vera's phone lit up. It was Derrick. She heard a subsequent rattle of knocks on the storm door and again on the front door downstairs. Adelia darted out of Vera's room, flew down the stairs and threw open the door. There, she found

Derrick, holding a convenience store bag bloated with medical supplies.

"Hurry, please!" Adelia begged before she raced back up the stairs.

Adelia draped the bloody blanket back over her daughter as Derrick clamored up the stairs, bag rustling beside him. Only Vera's head and arms were exposed. Clumps of red towels sat bundled on her arms.

Derrick froze the moment he saw Vera. There she laid, bloodied and lifeless, staring into nothing. He almost thought she was a corpse until he spotted her shallow breath.

Adelia broke him out of his daze. "Vera said you went to med school! Please, *please* help my baby!" She almost broke down completely, "She's *dyin'*!"

Derrick stammered, "She – I – *what*? I ...." He zipped up again. Perhaps it was best, he figured, that Adelia did not know the full truth. Instead, he pulled out cleaning wipes and packets of gauze pads. "Just keep pressure!" He ordered and went to Vera's side. With a careful voice, he announced loud and clear, "Vera! This is Derrick. I'm going to fix you up, okay?"

Vera's eyes drifted to Derrick and drifted away. Her mind was too sloppy to be embarrassed or care. He had a hollow, distant ring in his voice. A couple of her mother's tears pattered onto her face as she kept pressure.

"She's responding," Derrick noted. "That's good." He placed the bag on the side of the bed and ripped open the cleaning wipe. "Ms. Florence, when'd this happ– *How'd* this happen?"

"Not even a full hour ago, I found her like this," Adelia responded. "She was screaming and I came in finding her like this!"

Derrick wanted to ask what dream Vera had but figured that was probably a stupid question. He prepped the cleaning wipe and dug out some rubber gloves to pop on as he said, "Let me see how bad one of her arms are. You'll wipe it down to clean it, okay?"

Adelia removed one of the clumps. Derrick slightly gagged at the sight. The gash was deep and dark, it started to flood again.

"Put it back! Put it back!" Derrick fought to keep his dinner down.

Adelia replaced the towel, confused.

Derrick astonished, "She's going to have to get stitches. Those are some *deep* cuts!"

"Can't you do it?" Adelia asked, flummoxed.

Vera blinked slowly, listening to everything. Everyone sounded far away. The pain swallowed her whole.

Derrick sighed, frustrated. He pulled out his phone and tapped his TwipSearch bar. He typed "treat a slit wrist" as he muttered, "Let me check something."

Suicide hotline numbers populated the page. Even the Twip mascot, a mint lime bird, popped up on the side of the screen with a frown and box of tissues. A soft colored bubble read over the bird, "Want to talk? I'm confidential." Derrick scrolled down the page until he landed on a link to a medical college titled "Treating deep cuts on arms and wrists." He tapped on it and instructed Adelia on what to do.

"You're keeping pressure, good. We're gonna have to work quick on the next part." Derrick pocketed the phone and said, "I'm going to lift the towel. You clean it with those wipes and I'm going to then put down this gauze." He opened a gauze pad and laid the blanche, shiny square of cotton down in easy reach for Adelia. He checked his phone once more and fetched from the bag a roll of bandages. Breaking the plastic seal, he continued, "Then you're going to wrap up her arm with this bandage here. Wrap it *tightly* around that gauze. Got it?" He placed the roll down on the crumpled plastic, out of the way of blood.

Adelia nodded and readied herself. Vera rattled out a light cough.

Holding his hands ready, Derrick said, "Ok, on my count, we switch hands on the towel. One ... two ... three... Switch!"

Adelia lifted her hands and Derrick pressed down. With her hands padded with prints of blood from the towel, she pulled out new cleaning wipes. They stained orange around her fingertips.

"Good, good," Derrick praised, trying to keep his food down again. The metal, heavy smell of blood nauseated him almost as worse as the sight. "Now, I'm going to move the towel. Get that gauze there." Adelia picked up the gauze with her free hand, Derrick nodded, "Good. I'm going to yank the towel up, you clean and slap that gauze down. When you do, wrap it up. Ok? Here we go ... One ... two ... three ... Go!"

Derrick yanked up the heavy towels and Adelia speed-cleaned the wound on Vera's closest wrist. The blood wouldn't stop coming. She barely managed to get a clear outline of the gash when she slapped down the pad of gauze and wrapped up Vera's arm. The pad's center darkened as she wrapped the blood-streaked gauze around it. From what she could see, the gash extended from Vera's wrist to the middle of her forearm.

As Vera watched through her slow drifting eyes, she knew in her murky mind she never wanted to sleep again. She just couldn't.

Derrick and Adelia patched up Vera's other arm. Derrick offered Adelia some gloves but she passed. He changed gloves and they applied a second, clean layer of gauze.

"Looks like we're done," said Derrick. He collected the spent wipes and gloves. "I'm going to throw this away, okay? Where's the bathroom?"

"Down the hall on the left," aided Adelia. "And, Mr. Ma?"

He cracked a light smile, "Just call me 'Derrick'."

"Derrick," Adelia corrected herself, "thank you. Thank you for saving Vera." Tears bubbled up again but she fought them back down.

Derrick nodded, "No problem. Let me throw these out and I'll be on my way." He left the room.

Alone with her daughter, Adelia went to Vera's closet

and fished out a pink blanket from the top shelf. She returned to the bed and pulled the yellow blanket to the floor. Adelia then threw the crumpled wet towels into the yellow blanket and bundled it all together. She set the reddening lump aside and with a sharp flap, Adelia laid the pink blanket over Vera's battered body. She kissed Vera's forehead, her lips jutted into a painful frown. At the return of Derrick's heavy footsteps, Adelia stilled her face to something close to neutral.

Derrick walked back into the room, ungloved and with freshly washed arms. He complimented Vera, "You held in there! You'll get better soon. You won't have to come into the shop for the rest of this week and next week, okay?"

Adelia asked, "Are you sure?"

Derrick replied, "She has sick days, this is what they're there for." He checked the time, it was beyond late. "I'm going to head on out. Let me know how Vera is doing?" Derrick looked at Vera once more. He muttered to himself, "All this from a *dream*. Geez."

Adelia nodded, "Thank you, Derrick. Thank you so much. Let me know if there is anything you need. *Anything*."

Derrick waved off the offer, "I'm good. Just get Vera back on her feet soon. I'm off." He left Vera's room and thudded down the stairs.

Vera and Adelia heard the door swing open and close. Adelia sighed as she looked over her daughter. This was the worst she ever saw dream traveling. Her personal experience was so limited. The worst she had done was discover a teacher's desk in a dream and woke up holding an answer key for a test she was nervous about and that was by chance, not by practice. Victoria and Addie warned her of the bad and heinous in dream traveling but Adelia thought the time trick could get them out the worst of it. How wrong she was.

Vera's eyes drifted to meet her mother's. She dryly croaked, "Water? ... Ibuprofen?"

Without pause, Adelia rushed to her room across the hall. The master bedroom was large and neat, a queen-sized bed filled the center of the room. She had a black, diamond pattern headboard and a small, round nightstand beside it. In the drawer sat a small white bottle filled with cramp and headache medicine. Adelia plucked an empty cup from the tall purpleheart dresser against the wall and dashed to the bathroom to fill it. Before she filled it all the way, she noticed the bloodprint she left. She dumped out the water and washed her hands, the cup, and the medicine bottle. Orange-red swirled down the drain. She then filled the cup again and took everything into Vera's room, careful not to spill a single drop.

Adelia sat everything on the uneven floor beside Vera's bed. She popped open the medicine bottle and shook out three brown tablets. With care, Adelia lifted Vera's head and parted her child's dirt stained lips to slip in the tablets, one by one. Adelia then picked up the water and brought it to Vera's lips next.

Vera couched the tablets in her cheek to accept the

first sip to clear her throat. She coughed a terrible fit but the tablets stayed put. Her throat cleared enough now, Vera accepted the second sip, swallowing the tablets and all. It pained her to do so but so did everything else.

"Anything else?" Adelia asked. "Do you want to watch anything to take your mind off the pain?"

Vera spoke clearer but pain still infiltrated her tone, "Yes."

"Okay," Adelia nodded. "Do you want me to watch it with you?"

"...Yes." Vera didn't want to be alone, especially not now.

Adelia sat the cup down, "Okay, baby."

She went back to her room. On Adelia's bed was her tablet laid against a plump, marigold pillow. She grabbed both and returned to Vera's room. Beside Vera, Adelia placed down the pillow on the floor and flipped out her tablet case's prop to set it between them on Vera's bed.

"Do you want to watch your show?" Adelia asked as she woke the tablet and unlocked it. There were a few apps but the screen was mostly bare. The wallpaper bore an impressionist painting of a white crane about to take flight from a shallow lake.

"...Yes," Vera croaked.

"Ok, let me set that up and we will be on our way," Adelia promised as she went to Twip Search and typed in "Mystery Pop Pop episodes". In seconds, the page was filled with a list of links but the second one was directly to the episode list. Tapping it, a condensed mobile site popped up.

Adelia rose up from the pillow to turn off the overhead bedroom light. She returned to her seat and tapped the link for "Episode 1, Season 1". Adelia laid her head on Vera's mattress, mindful of Vera's arm and together, they watched.

Chapter IV

Vera suffered over the next three days. Sleep terrified her, her throat still seized with prickles whenever she spoke and her wounds besieged her every move. Adelia fixed her honey tea every morning but it soothed little. Vera rarely left the bed, only when Adelia changed the bloody sheets and for the bathroom, to which she traveled with wobbly footsteps. Each bandage change was a mess, blood still poured and healing was slow. Adelia had to change Vera's sheets at least three times since bandaging her up the first time.

To stay awake, Vera would blast loud music in her headphones and wash her face with cold water. She started warming the water a little when memories of The Hunter's grave flashed back. She tried to stroll past the bathroom a couple times but her wounds would punish her.

On the third day, Vera drifted off while watching a synthwave music video. She didn't know she was dreaming until she looked over her shoulder and saw Love. He kneaded her shoulders, taking away the pain. She was wrapped up in a thick blue blanket with silver tribal markings in front of a roaring fire. His calm smile and swirling eyes jarred her awake. Gasping for breath, Vera noticed all but her wrists were healed. No nicks, no prickles, her throat was clear. Her legs were fine, her ribs no longer ached with every drawn breath. The slashes of her scars laid fine but twinged when she flexed her fingers.

Renewed, Vera slipped out of bed and tried to get dressed. The sun hung bright in the near afternoon sky, hazy humid air caked the room. With cupped hands, Vera sifted through her clothes pile, careful to not use her fingers. She drew out a long, black skirt and a simple navy tank. Draping them aside, Vera dug a little more. She didn't want to go out with her bandages exposed. Some painful twinges later, Vera ferreted out some silver splattered arm warmers. She hardly wore them for the small bleach stain inside the elbow but they covered her bandages so on they went.

As Vera dug around underneath her bed with her foot, she dredged out a slew of chunky platforms. Among them, three matched but only one was a slip-on pair. Short, wedged platforms with a star cut through the heel. Vera propped the shoes upright and slid into them, her height lifted by a couple inches.

Satisfied with her outfit, Vera visited her closet to pull out a tan canvas shopping bag from the back. She laced it onto her shoulder and returned to her bed. Vera scooped out her keys out of a pair of pants crumpled in front of her bed and unhooked her chain wallet to shovel them into her skirt's pocket. Prickles danced throughout her wrist as she used her fingers to unhook the steel latch of her chain wallet. She paused until the needling went away. Then she collected her phone from the bed and left to set out into the world.

First order of business: go to the convenience store and procure as many energy drinks as she could carry. She no longer wanted to chance sleep. The last dream was pleasant but what about the next? As Vera slogged down the street, cloistered by the heat and humidity, Love slipped to mind. She wondered if this was fair to him but the brutality of The Hunter flashed to mind. Vera's heart leapt in her chest at the thought of all The Hunter could do to Love. Severance was best.

At the store, Vera relished the chilling grasp of the frosty air conditioner. The muggy heat had started to throb her wounds. Off in the distance, Vera spotted an employee straightening her name tag on her blue polo shirt in the makeup and hosiery section, "Anaiyah" stickered on her plastic tag in crooked letters. The young woman donned dark bronze skin, fresh cornrows and a full plate of makeup caked on her face. Vera hurried over before the employee could duck her.

"Excuse me?" Vera asked once she was close enough not to yell. "Could you help me?"

With a trained smile, Anaiyah replied, "Sure, what do you need help with?"

"I wanted to get a couple cases of energy drinks. Can you help carry a case or two?" The subtle throb of her arms distracted her a little but she remained focused. At least enough not to wince during the occasional sharp stab.

Anaiyah looked at Vera's arms, Vera looked down with her. It was obvious the store attendant thought Vera fine and healthy, just prissy and stuck up but she nodded and answered, "Sure, everything is in aisle thirteen."

Vera followed Anaiyah past scores of tall aisles. Aisle thirteen hailed a colorful hall of drinks, powder mixes and drinkware. Stacked in the middle of the aisle were the energy drinks. Small cans, big cans, glass bottles, the selection was countless.

"Which one would you like?" Anaiyah presented.

Vera rarely drank anything harder than storeroom coffee. She once had a five-hour bottle to finish a term paper that left her wired and hyper for a day and a half. What she remembered most was the crash, she slept like the dead. Love was in the dream she had, looking into a box made of sand on the beach. It was filled with clouds and strange apples with jeweled cores kept tumbling out. Her mother woke her up when sand and clouds of cotton had started to fall from under her covers.

A case of cans had caught Vera's eye. The case was stark black, with smeared white light spread over the center of the box. The quadruplet of cans carried the photonegative effect of the box, they were silver with smeared black light spread over the center of each can. Under the rim of each can bore, "Wake Up The Night" in blasted lettering. Midnight Suns, one of the strongest brands on the market. They made the news a year ago about the over-potency of their formula after a college student collapsed from three cans but nothing came of that. Nothing Vera cared about. She wanted peace from her night terrors.

"Two packs of those," Vera pointed out.

Anaiyah picked up the two heavy packs and walked them up to the front. Vera spied from the employee's slumped shoulders that the cases might be a bit of trouble getting home. She shook away the worry and prepared her wallet as she followed Anaiyah to the line of registers up front.

Each case clanked loud as Anaiyah set them down on the beat up, navy blue counter. Irritation trickled onto her face as she rang up the items. The chunky register blipped each scan and displayed the price on the card reader.

With her trained smile, Anaiyah informed, "That will be fifteen thirty-four. Cash or credit?"

Vera replied, "Credit," and entered her card into the reader. Pressing the credit soft key, a twinge made her wince. She hoped the store attendant didn't see. Vera drew a loose wiggle line as her signature and took off her bag to open it on the counter. "I have this bag here," she said.

Anaiyah picked up the two cartons and placed them in the crumpled down bag. She saw Vera wince on the card machine but she was too irritated to care. She just wanted Princess out of her store. With a swift updraw of the stitched handles, Anaiyah said, "Let me get your receipt and you are good to go." She snatched off the spat-out receipt and threw it in the bag, "Thank you, please have a nice day."

Vera returned Anaiyah's plastic smile as she drew the bag onto her shoulder. With a clear heft of the bag off the counter, the straps sliced into her shoulder and gave her wound on that arm a deep twinge. She nodded goodbye and headed out the sliding doors, back into the brisk heat.

On the walk back, Vera had to adjust herself several times. The heavy bag burrowed into her shoulder and the sweltering heat aided no help. Eager to get home, Vera never stopped trudging along to switch shoulders. She tried to jump the straps to a better position but they would dig in further from recoil. When they bit into her shoulder like a vice, Vera stopped under the nearest shady tree. The aluminum cans clattered as she slid the bag onto the ground. She rotated and shook her arm. It was nothing The Hunter ever gave her but the sandy throbs burned all the same. Vera stepped over the bag to thread it onto her better shoulder. She only had a block left but the pain and heat made it feel an infinity away. Plus, the strap ached her again.

The remainder of the walk left her soggy and beat. Her

wounds pounded from strain and sweat. Her shoulder stung. She slopped through the gate and hurried to the door. The air was so stuffy, she could hardly feel herself breathe. At her door, she leaned against the open storm door as the bag toppled from her shoulder. Vera tried to use the heel of her foot and the crick of her elbow to slow the fall to the porch. Daggers of pain bit under her bandages as the bag clanged to the ground. She leapt from the noise, half-expecting a shallow pool to seep out from underneath the bag. The cement stayed dry.

Fishing out her keys was a task, as they sat deep in her pockets. She tried to paw them out, but they kept slipping from her fingertips. Vera then tried to peck at them with grouped fingers, and the twinges of pain were sharp and quick. When the keyring hooked onto her ring finger proper, she whisked them out and fumbled to the correct key. Desperate to leave the heat, Vera opened the door. Her jaw dropped in a silent wail as she fought to turn the key. The humidity made the lock sticky and difficult. She tumbled to her knees over the threshold. Her arms jabbered with agony as she held them close. The cold air embraced her clammy skin but the heat still roared at her back. Hissing out an airy whine, the storm door tapped against her heels and bag. Vera looked up at her keys still hanging in the knob. They swayed in the light wind. Vera weighed the option of leaving them in the door to retrieve later but she didn't want to answer any questions that would bring. She braced herself and pulled the keys out the lock. They popped out far easier than they turned.

Vera slid them back into her pocket and stared at the canvas bag, lost in thought. Her shoulders couldn't take another go with the straps, they felt cleaved enough.

A haggard sigh drifted out of Vera. She scooted to the bag and threaded her head through the straps to pick it up. Vera got to her feet, left foot, then right, bent over and unwilling. Her back strained, the bag bit into the back of her neck as she stood upright. She staggered from the new weight against her, the storm door clattered shut. Her neck felt awful but at least it wasn't her arms. Vera kicked the front door closed and hurried up the stairs before her neck gave out. Every tug of weight felt like wire against her spine.

Her bedroom bore the hallmarks of outside but without the cutting sun. Vera dropped the bag off by her bed and crashed into her pillow. There, she stayed, waiting for the pain to subside. She needed enough strength to hide the cans. Her mother would have her head if she found them. Adelia chewed out Vera when she woke her from the five-hour drink crash, there's no way Vera wanted a repeat of that.

Cotton candy tumbleweeds rumbled past her legs. Vera jerked awake from the sight. She had drifted off again. Pain still encased her but the terror of falling asleep was greater. Vera slid off the bed and pulled out a can. Heavy and uncomfortably warm, Vera propped the can between her thighs and stopped. It had a finger tab. Vera threw her head back, tears of her future agony burned her eyes. With a swift movement, she pried a fingernail under the tab until she could fit a finger and ripped the can open. She tried to stifle her cry for mercy but a quick sob broke from her. She shriveled into a ball. Warm drink sloshed over, Vera sucked on the can to prevent further spills. The drink had a fruity smell, the artificial sweetness barely masked the husky chemical taste behind it. Vera paused to get used to the flavor, her face ticked from the bitterness.

But the fatigue burned away. She savored the buzz behind her eyes and the rush of her heartbeat. Vera drank down another slug. Never would she dare sleep again.

※

Vera didn't sleep a wink for the rest of the week. She adjusted quickly to the taste of the Midnight Suns. A little went a long way so she was certain her well wouldn't dry too soon. The drink taught her how much she could have and how much she couldn't handle. Her skin painfully prickled with sweat if she slurped too much. To prevent wasting any open cans, she would pour each can she freshly opened into a sports bottle she found under her bed. Vera could tell it would taste better chilled but beggars couldn't be choosers. She couldn't risk her mother discovering.

During the day, Vera would take a decent slug every couple hours, sometimes an in-between sip if she felt a crash was coming. At night, she took down more, the closest gulp she could take before her skin needled. She stayed in her room; she didn't want to risk appearing *too* lively around her mother. When Adelia was home, Vera would stay in bed, watching fast paced movies or listen to eurotrash and EDM with the headphones cranked loud. When Adelia was away, Vera would burn her energy throughout the house: running up and down the stairs, playing bullet hell video games. Her world was a blur of hyper-speed. When her wrists still ached, she would take some ibuprofen and wash it down with more Midnight Suns. Vera knew this wasn't her best plan but it was the only one she had.

On Tuesday, Vera waited for her mother to leave. She wanted to try going to work. The lack of sleep made her woozy and fuzzy-headed but she still wanted to try. Getting dressed still was a challenge, since the lack of sleep had slowed her healing to a near standstill. In the hour it took for her to get dressed, her pants gave the most trouble, and the twinges of pain were the worst that day. After she slid on her arm warmers and shoes, Vera searched her closet. With a bit of sifting and digging, out came a drawstring bag with a zig zag stripe down the middle, crumpled and flat. A handout from a fall festival last year. She brought it back to her bed to put her sports bottle in. It was silver and lime with a black nub, a faint waterline rippled and sloshed against the bottle as it rolled and slipped into her bag. It was a quarter full of the last can, and Vera treated it like the precious resource that it was. Maybe, maybe if the world didn't swirl or tilt too much, she would get some more after her visit to YinYue.

Vera threw the bag onto her shoulders and stumbled from the momentum. Her brain felt slower than her hands, and it took a moment for her to recognize that she was indeed falling and she needed to catch herself. It gave her a heavy knock against the wall but she propped herself back up, right as rain and ready to go.

The walk to the bus stop wasn't too bad. Sun haze shone through the drifting veil of grey. The humidity finally broke, the air breezed by refreshing and warm. The gentle gusts and chattering birds rejuvenated Vera. Never had she felt so run down, the world felt like a sloppy painting she waded through. *I shoulda ... man ... I shoulda took a swig before I left*, drifted through Vera's soggy brain as she swayed a little with the wind. Leaned against the warm pole of the bus stop, Vera wanted to sit. She wanted to sleep.

The free bus pulled around the corner. Vera couldn't tell if she waited long or drifted off. It rumbled down the street and whined to a greasy stop in front of her. The doors swung apart, the rumble resonating loud in Vera's head, and she got on. Having no clue if it was the correct line, Vera plopped down into a side window seat and tried not to drift off. It was late morning and the bus was quiet and cool. Vera almost slipped off a couple times but the hard stops, clanging chimes, and the occasional loud patron jarred her awake. Through her bleary eyes, she saw YinYue pulling up in the distance. She pressed the dingy orange chime tape with her elbow and tried to sort herself. The world was such a cacophony of senses. She wanted quiet. She wanted sleep.

Vera waited for the bus to come to a full stop before she got up. The head rush that met her almost sat her down again but she powered through. Vera collected herself with a quick drawn breath and sauntered as confident as she could off the bus, hopeful she wouldn't faceplant onto the pavement.

With a sound tap on the sidewalk, a hint of pride glimmered through her fog as she veered her way across the parking lot towards YinYue. She was sure she had a straight stride but she drifted a bit in her walk.

Derrick was behind the counter putting away a returned album when he spotted Vera drifting in. Surprise bloomed across his face. He bounded up over to her, "Holy–! You're better already?"

The pounding speakers drowned her mind. Vera squinted but flattened her face to hide her disturbance. She replied with a bleary smile, "I dreamed myself better."

Derrick gave her an unsure eye. She appeared drained and worse for wear. "Really?"

The heavy metal blaring from the speakers made Vera a little wobbly. Before it was obvious, she said, "I'mma … I'mma be in the back." Her voice was slow and worn.

Derrick nodded and stepped aside. He watched her drift past him, astonished. Just last week, she was at death's door. Now, she was up and moving again … albeit a bit off. He wanted to trail behind her to ask more of her condition but a pink haired girl with spiked boots and midnight skin wanted to be rung up.

Vera stumbled her way to the cot. The music overpowered her senses and the world tilted and shifted about too much for her liking. It didn't even fully register with her that she had fallen onto the cot until she felt the taut canvas under her palms. She slipped off the drawstring backpack and drew it into her lap slowly. Then, she sat still. The music pulsed through her, she couldn't sort out her soggy brain. Thoughts dragged across her head, lost before they could reach a destination. She pried open the bag and fished out her bottle to take a long sip. A soft buzz lit up behind her eyes but she didn't perk up like before. The effect hit her less and less now. Even in her hazy state, that concerned her. She didn't want to go to sleep.

To wake herself up, Vera lifted off the cot. Another head rush met her. She stuck out her arms and stumbled into balance. She figured the pounding music would keep her awake, so she gathered her bottle into the bag, laced it onto her shoulders and walked out into the store.

The overhead music faded to trip hop. Derrick spotted Vera leaving the storeroom from his perch behind the counter. He folded his arms and cocked his head. Her footing was unsteady and she kept drifting to the side in her stride. Vera bumped into countless things, her hip clipped a pyramid of travel amps sitting on a table. She would have toppled them too if a customer didn't stop her. Vera appeared slow and clueless as she apologized. Moving away, she bumped into a standee for record players. She was beyond off.

Before she could teeter into something else, Derrick flew down from behind the counter and tapped her on the shoulder. Into her ear, he beckoned, "Come with me," and led her back into the storeroom with a firm grip on her arm.

Vera blathered out, confused and flustered, "Wha- what's happenin'? I swear I'm fine." She could barely keep up with his pace, she clipped herself but he held firm as he brought her along.

Derrick stood Vera inside and leaned against the jamb to keep an eye on the store. "I'm not stupid and I'm going to ask once: what are you *on*?"

Vera blanked at the question. "What? Wha'd –"

"I know you too well to *think* you're doing something stupid or worth firing you for but I'll ask one more time, last chance: What are you *on*? There's no way this is dream *anything*. I've been around enough to know this. I've never messed around but I sure as hell can *recognize* it. No answer, no job. Bad answer, no job. Go."

Blood racing, Vera tumbled out, "Nah ... not doin' ... I'm- Midnight Suns!" She knew that sentence wasn't right, she threw up a finger to parse out the sentence again, "I'm ... I'm drinkin' Midnights."

Derrick wasn't moved. He spat, "You don't drink that shi–"

"It *true*!" Vera defended. Her mind raced through molasses to string the right words together. "But I don' ... I don't be havin' a lot." She slipped off her bag and presented it. "Only a lil' an' that's it. Nothin' ... nothin' else. I *swear.*"

Derrick snatched the bag and ripped it open as she finished. He pulled out the sports bottle, flattened and folded the bag to check for anything else, and unscrewed the top. He sniffed the bottle and took a test sip. He recoiled, the energy drink was warm, flat and strong. "How much of this stuff – no, how *long* have you been drinking this? I've never seen you with anything stronger than coffee!"

Vera thought for a while, waiting for her mind to catch up and do the math.

Impatient, Derrick repeated, "How *long*? You're bumping into things like a zomb–"

"A week?" Vera guessed. "Or more? Definitely after y'all found me."

Derrick eyes' widened. He took a quick scan of the store before returning to Vera. "You haven't slept for a *week*?"

Vera snapped her fingers, "Bingo."

Derrick rolled his eyes and smeared his hand along his face. Midnight Suns was strong stuff, he used to down three a week back in med school, five during finals and midterms. He once prepared instant coffee with it, he never tried that again. Derrick went into his bathroom and turned on the sink, "I'm dumping this."

Panic flared throughout Vera, she tried to get the bottle away. "Stop! I *need* it!"

Derrick turned, beyond done with her foolishness.

"What for? Vera, you are *not* thinking straight. You went through some scary shit, I'll give you *that*. But this is *not* the way to handle it. It's going down the drain, story *over*." He flooded the sink with cherry brown and washed out the rest.

Overwhelmed and bedraggled, Vera argued, "The Hunter is *terrifying*. I nearly *died*."

Derrick screwed the cap back on and checked the bag once more before returning the bottle, "Vera, giving yourself a collapse or heart failure isn't a much better option *either*. You need to *sleep*. The Hunter is in *your* head. That's *your* domain–"

"I can't!"

"Try!" Derrick snipped. "Did you plan to literally never sleep *again*? You may think you're running away from him but he's just wearing you down on the outside. Can't you use positive dream symbols to fight him off?"

Vera sank to the floor, defeated and misunderstood. "My brain don't *work* that way."

"Vera, you're a *mess* right now, get it to work that way. Think of Care Bears, kittens, whatever."

Derrick peered out the storeroom. A customer ready to make a purchase waved at him by the counter. An old man with weathered sable skin holding a jazz vinyl. Derrick directed Vera, "Get some freakin' sleep. Cot's right there. Do it." He then exited the storeroom and closed the door shut. Muffled, Vera heard, "Ready to buy? I'll ring you up right here."

Sunk and hopeless, Vera knew Derrick was right. She

couldn't outrun The Hunter forever. Vera pulled out her phone. Unlocking it, she went to her Twip Search bar and said, "Hey Twip."

The search bar flashed green, "Speak now" floated down.

"How does the killer die in 'Mass Graves Two'?" Vera asked. She remembered the second poster from the end of the movie, how it was supposed to be the end of the killer and the story.

A list of links popped up. A cursory glance showed that *Mass Graves 2* was shelved because the first movie flopped badly. Dread filled her now, there was no straightforward method to rid The Hunter. Defeated and tired, she simply had no choice but to face him and on her own.

Pocketing her phone, Vera dragged herself to the cot. She sighed as she laid down and tried to fall asleep.

※

She was back in the forest – in the clutches of The Hunter. She donned a robin red top and billowy white pants that were the bells of flowers. Balanced on a thin, horizontal tree, Vera leaned against a strip of rope that felt as stiff and sturdy as a wide board. Pressed behind her hips was a wooden plank, white-washed and prickled with splinters. Shimmering, golden lines replaced the long slashes on her arms, she had full use of her trembling hands again.

From the distant ground, The Hunter stared with a

crazed, toothy smile. He appeared far away but felt eye to eye to her. Even his voice sounded close.

"My word," The Hunter marveled. "Aren't you perfect? Are you just like me?"

Vera yelled her response but nothing came out, her voice was gone.

Suddenly, The Hunter was close to her, his head at her navel. A lurid smile drifted upon his face as he produced a hammer from nowhere. He gave her left hip a single, light tap that boomed like a nail gun, driving in a double sized coffin nail. She roared out a silent scream. A beautiful ribbon of blood rolled down underneath the nail.

The Hunter gave another tap in the center of her hip, and one more on her right hip, three altogether. Firmly attached to the plank behind her, Vera couldn't help but to curl her hands and erupt out in muted screams. She couldn't double over. She had to take in the agony upright. Vera gripped the rope above her but her hands couldn't grasp. They flopped to her side as The Hunter stood back to admire his handiwork. Then, he disappeared.

The gold lines on her arms started to dribble down into her palms, they felt like rushing creeks of sand. But they were painless. Desperate to get out, Vera cupped her hands over the left nail. She pulled her shaking hands away, drawing out the nail. It slid out, slow and excruciating until it tinkered onto the ground as if falling onto a metal plate. The pain disappeared.

Sucking in gasps of relieved air, Vera pulled out the

middle nail. It slid out just as awful as the first, as if little rusted one-way barbs jutted out. Another tinker, and the nail was gone. As was the pain. One more to go.

The third one gave up the same fight, Vera wanted so much to give up and give in to The Hunter but the fear kept her going. Gold soaked her palms and collected on the tips of her fingers as she pulled. On the third tinker, Vera watched the nail splash into sand as it struck the ground. She heaved deep breaths, her arms streaked with gold. Vera blew on them and dusted the gold off. The shimmer plumed into the air, and a scream rattled in her ear.

"WHAT ARE YOU DOI–"

Vera woke up with a start. Sweating and terrified, she patted her hips and arms. Nothing ached, nothing burned, she was whole again. Vera ripped off her arm warmers and unfixed her bandages. Twirling them off her arms, the blood-absorbed wraps revealed clean, whole skin.

The storeroom door clicked open. All was quiet, only Derrick's booted footsteps as he came in with the register's money bag tucked under his arm. End of the day.

"Derrick!" Vera called out. "I'm healed!" She sprang up from the cot, head clear and adrenaline draining away. She presented her bare arms, "I ... I'm better now."

He stepped forth and examined each arm. No nicks, no marks, no scars, nothing at all. He was at a loss for words, his jaw hinged and bobbled as he tried to speak.

"How .... You ... you dreamt yourself ... *completely* better?"

Vera smiled, "I guess so." She slipped her arms out of his hands. Her smile faded, "The Hunter struck again, though."

"You defeated him, right?" Derrick couldn't wait to hear the story.

Vera sighed with a solemn shake. "I barely escaped." She tapped her temple, "Still in there."

"Oh," Derrick's shoulders slumped. Quickly, he added, "But this is something! This can help you get the jump on him! Right?"

Vera's face twisted, she already discounted the thought. Her nose scrunched up, "I don't think it works that way."

Frustration bubbled under Derrick's voice, "Vera, you're having the same nightmares again and again. Either you gotta defeat it or get over it. That's the only way past them. And with you, you *really* need to find a solution." He turned around and went to push aside the record crate.

Vera sat back down on the cot, her head swirling in rumination. Usually, Vera's nightmares went away on their own or she would become more powerful than the thing scaring her. But The Hunter held her terror, good and sound.

The safe clanked shut. Derrick spun the dial and slid back the crate. He stood up and asked, "Are you ready to leave?"

Derrick drove Vera home. The ride was more melodic than usual, Derrick played softer rock and some dark wave in the hope Vera could rest a little more. She seemed well but he wanted to be sure. Vera stayed awake, watching the city blur by.

With the truck parked and quiet behind Adelia's car, Derrick and Vera walked to the door. Vera relished her nimble fingers as she picked out her keys and opened the door.

Adelia sat anxious and scrolling through her tablet on the couch. She leapt up as soon as she heard the door click. Upon hearing familiar bootsteps, she raced over and yanked Vera into her arms. She covered her daughter in boundless kisses.

"I thought you were gone!" Adelia sniffed. "Oh, thank you, God," she praised before covering Vera in more kisses. Then, she spotted Derrick, who carried a baffled smile. "Where'd you find her?"

"At work," he replied, awkward and unsure. "Should I go?"

Adelia looked down at her daughter and back at Derrick. She shook her head, "No, no, please come in."

Derrick nodded and stepped through, closing the yellow door. Adelia moved back with Vera firm in her arms.

Muffled by her mother's shoulder, Vera declared, "Ma! I'm doin' better now–"

"I thought you disappeared!" Adelia agonized. Her voice broke but she kept back her tears. Adelia squeezed Vera tighter and showered her with kisses again. To Derrick, she tried to explain, "Our family ... this trait .... Some – some of our ancestors would use it to escape slavery. They wanted freedom so much they would disappear in their beds. My grandmother would tell me the story of our great, great aunt, Bedelia."

Vera looked up. "Ma, that story?" She briefly explained to Derrick, "She was a Buffalo Soldier. Ma's told this story a million times."

Derrick still couldn't settle his confusion. "I – I thought they were all men."

Vera jumped in before her mother could reply, "So did they. She snuck in."

"Vera!" Adelia chided lightly. "May I finish? Bedelia could dream travel but go to actual places with it and *stay* there. Grandmother said Bedelia would find herself in strange places all the time. Sometimes it would benefit her ... and sometimes it didn't.

One of the last times she was seen, it was by one of her fellow soldiers, who wrote my family a letter. He said that Bedelia was sleeping sound in their tent. Then he saw her disappear in pieces until she disappeared completely. Never to be seen again. His commander didn't believe him and everyone thought he helped 'Matthew' – Bedelia's soldier name – go awol. He wrote to us to clear his conscience. He thought he was going mad from the stress of war.

My grandmother regretted no one ever writing back to him. The poor man told us something important and we just let him suffer with the truth. Our family doubled down on the secret instead." Looking down at Vera, Adelia admitted, "I honestly have no clue if Vera is the only one left. There could be more but slavery broke up our family and we suppressed the truth of our abilities so much, there just isn't any way of knowing." She laid her head upon her daughter, "When I came home and didn't see Vera in bed, I immediately feared the worst."

Derrick was still in a state of wonder, this was so much to take in. He shook his head to refresh his mind, "Wow ... this is ... wow, certainly something ...."

"I'm sure this all sounds confusing," said Adelia.

Derrick doled out a breathy laugh, "You're tellin' *me*. In all the time I have known Vera, never in all my years would I have suspected *any* such thing. Vera, you are really something .... But I'm glad you're alright." He joked, "Dream of ponies and cotton candy from now on, okay?"

Smiles crackled onto Vera and Adelia's faces. Adelia kissed Vera on the head twice. Oh, how her heart swelled with joy at the sight of her daughter safe in her arms.

Vera returned a small kiss to her mother's cheek and chuckled, "I'll try."

With a sound clap of his hands, Derrick announced, "I'm going to head out. Sleep well, ok, Vera?"

Vera nodded. "Thanks, Derrick." Adelia snuggled into her.

He waved, "No problem. You sleep well, too, Ms. Florence." He got the door and left, quietly closing it behind him.

Adelia snuggled Vera once more.

※

That night, Vera and Adelia slept in Adelia's room. Curled together in bed under a blue summer blanket, Vera slept sound against her mother's cheek.

In Vera's dream, she was in a room made of dark blue diamonds. The jagged wall, the tall table, the chairs with pinprick legs. Vera sat in the center of the room playing with blocks made of tarnished brass wires. They were not full blocks, only outlines and every time she stacked the blocks, they always tumbled through each other, corner first. Vera plumed with frustration every time as she tried to stack them again and again.

"Baby girl," a man called out, his voice aged and weary. A working man's voice. "You need to do it right."

The man stood before her. Bald and deep copper skin, tired, hazel eyes and round cheeks. His shoulders were built and slumped from years of work and toil. Hints of gray speckled about his trimmed goatee. The man resonated comfort – he was her father, the dream world version of him.

"Daddy!" Vera perked up, her voice that of a child. She held out the blocks, brimming with eagerness, "Show me how to do it!"

Her father chuckled, "Oh, Vera. Baby girl, you're rushing. Don't rush. We'll get ice cream soon."

Vera plopped her hands into her little lap. She smiled and bounced, "Mama needs to come!"

The father's smile waned. He faded away.

Sorrow bled into her heart, Vera started to tear up.

Behind her, her father scooped her up into his arms, "I'm here, I'm here, baby girl." Holding her close and rocking her gently, he sang to her, "Daddy's little girl," over and over.

Vera nestled her head against his chest. He felt like mountain rocks. He always did, like an unfinished living statue. But she loved him. His skin was warm, his voice was kind.

Her father planted a soft kiss on her forehead. "Precious baby girl," he whispered.

Then she woke up.

It was morning. Her mother was still asleep, head tucked down. Vera felt the shadow of her father's kiss on her forehead. She propped up on one elbow and rocked her mother awake. Adelia creased open her eyes. Unbeknownst to her and her daughter, Adelia's eyes were covered in crinkled gold foil. They faded back to normal as she stirred a little more. As Adelia stretched, Vera spoke with blurry tongue.

"'Ey, Ma? I think I'mma go sleep in my room so you can get ready for work." A gaping yawn escaped her, she covered her mouth.

Hardly awake, Adelia muttered, "Sleep here."

Vera slid back down beside her mother and kissed her on the cheek. "Ma, I'm fine. I won't go nowhere, I promise." She slinked out her mother's bed and padded to her own room. Vera could hardly walk straight. Groggy from the absence of Midnight Suns in her system, Vera felt like she could sleep for years. She climbed into her own bed and drifted off again.

Her dream came quick.

Vera found herself in a house. It was bigger than the one she lived in, Vera could sense that. She was in the basement bedroom. The walls were painted a tired pastel blue, chunks and chips of drywall showed through between the cracks. The bedroom was plain, simple and long unused. Behind Vera was a window. Outside were thin, bare trees under a rolling overcast sky. Before her stood a wooden door, wide open. There laid the rest of the basement, cloaked in darkness. The most Vera could discern was the couple inches of smeared, mottled cement floor before it stretched into the void.

Vera looked over her shoulder. Sea water sloshed against the window. There was heavy flooding outside the house but inside, it was bone dry.

She returned to the doorway. She strained to make out whatever could be hidden in the darkness beyond. Faint shapes, maybe boxes and crates, but nothing certain. Her hair folded itself into two long cornrows. Lilies sprouted from each braid at the nape of her neck, their pistils dust blue.

As she stared into the darkness, The Hunter sprinted in towards her. Surprised and afraid, Vera balled her fists, crossed her arms and threw them aside. The house collapsed around The Hunter while passing through Vera.

When she blinked, Vera was atop the mountain of rubble. The only dry land among the choppy, growing floodwaters. She sensed the murky floodwaters were fathoms deep and her heart flared. She didn't want to drown. She could sense houses and neighborhoods under the currents. She didn't want to join them. But she could not feel any dread for The Hunter. He was no more.

Waves wiped over her red converses, she tipped back. The waves licked over them again. At the edge of her view, a black hurricane rotated into being just under the surface of the gray water. It bore a startling red eye as it streamed towards her, growing in size. Vera couldn't breathe. She was trapped in another bad dream.

Beside her, Love appeared. His dreads were held back with a thick silver spiral cuff and he wore a confident smile. Love stood atop the water as it lapped against her ankles.

Drown with me, he thought to her. His voice was low and deep, celestial and ethereal.

Vera rattled her head no, eyes wide with horror. The hurricane was close, only yards away. It looked like it could cover miles.

Love stood behind her and grasped her hands. He slipped his arms around her waist and laid his chin over her shoulder. *Drown with me.*

He tilted them backwards into the water, the hurricane inches away. Together, they sank like stones. Water rushed into Vera's lungs as she shut her eyes tight. The water disappeared when she opened them. They were side by side together in a lonesome movie theatre.

The sloped carpet floor was empty except for their two seats. Love couldn't take his eyes off Vera. Galaxies and nebulas swirled across his eyes as he kept his gaze. A soft smile curled upon his face when she looked at him.

Vera smiled back. "Are we watching a movie?"

Love nodded and looked ahead. Vera did the same. No screen on the wall, just a knocked-out wall and a bustling paper mâché city living before them, layered and thriving.

Fixated on the chugging taxis, milling crowds and chattering birds, Love kissed Vera on the temple. He then turned to her and gave her another on the cheek as she admired the city sights, a smile growing on her face. Love took her hand, Vera gave it a gentle squeeze. Love returned the same. Vera pecked him on the cheek and snuggled up against him. He laced an arm over her shoulder and held her close.

This was a pleasant dream.

Epilogue

Happy Sunday was in full swing. Lights off, luminated only by the early evening sun, a circle of chairs sat in the center of the store. Derrick was the eldest of the participants sitting in the ring, everyone else was a teen or a young adult. He sat facing the doors, engaged in the conversation around him. Vera rearranged the guitars on the far wall. Viper had seen one she liked, a clear blue Stratocaster, and asked for a couple sites to check out the basics of guitar playing. Vera thought it would be interesting to see what Viper would make of it.

In the circle, a chubby faced girl with rosy cheeks and light hair bubbled, "I saw this really cute girl at the market the other day. I wanted to talk to her but my dad was with me. Besides …," she trailed off. The girl picked at her cranberry nails, "You never know with people nowadays."

She waved away the thought, "I'm still not sure if I'm having a phase or whatever. Like, I like girls but I don't think I *like* girls, y'know what I mean?" She looked around, hopeful she didn't confuse anyone.

Around her, some sort of agreed, others didn't.

Across from her, a thin boy with wire glasses replied, "How? You seem to always go back and forth. Like, didn't you talk about wanting a boyfriend last time? What happened to that?"

The girl blinked, blindsided. "I still feel like that!" She joked, "I feel *strongly* about that." A small flood of laughter rolled through the circle. She chuckled herself and continued, "I just thought she was cute. Like ... I don't know." She gave up, plopping her hands onto her star-covered skirt. "I guess I like girls? But ... not as much as boys? I don't know how to explain it."

Before the bespectacled boy could reply, Derrick spoke out with ease, "I think get you." He leaned back, "I'm pretty sure I also like guys as well as girls. But there are days that are seventy-thirty, days that are fifty-fifty and days that are a hundred-hundred."

Some members chuckled, a couple whispered among themselves. Derrick usually focused conversation on everyone else, only from time to time did he focus it on himself. Old-comers knew Derrick was bi, as did Vera and Viper. There was a reason the card reader had the colors it did and why the golden cat always wore a blue, lavender and fuchsia paper hat every June.

Derrick looked around the circle with a smirk, "My

college dating days were cringey at best because I wasn't straight with myself." Several participants of the circle laughed at the accidental pun. Derrick was late to catch on but laughed heartily when he did.

A younger girl with three piercings in her left ear asked, "How did you figure that out?"

Derrick gave it some thought. "Hm ... I guess I just got older. I always thought I'd be married to a wife – y'know, what my family wanted and expected – but really, a decent husband doesn't sound too bad, either. I just don't want to marry an asshole. Already dated too many of those," he chuckled.

The girl with piercings spotted Vera hanging up a double neck guitar. She called out, "What about you, Vera?"

Vera fumbled the cherry guitar, clutching it to her chest. She whirled around, wide eyed. "Huh?"

"Guys, girls or both?" the girl asked with a teasing smile.

Vera stammered at the question. *Center of attention, great.*

Derrick chided lightly, "That's up to her, don't be intrusive."

The pierced girl looked at him, a bit taken aback. "But she's here every week, hovering around in the background. The least she could do is participate."

"She can do that because *I* say so." Derrick boasted playfully to the group, "My Chinese name is *Wang* Ma! That means I'm the *king* here," Laughter erupted in the circle, Derrick continued, "Vera's cool, that's why she's here. Besides," he looked to her. She was still frozen with stage fright. "I'm sure she knows the right person in her dreams."

Think the story is over?

It isn't.

There's still music to be made

Dreams to be had

Glass & Dreams

Book 1 & 2

A Tie-In Duology between:

Dreamer

The Glassman

TBD 2026/2027

Other works

Null (Void)

In Search of Amika

Kinetics

The Glassman

About the Author

MultiMind lives in Baltimore, Maryland. She tries to find time for her countless hobbies, from 3D printing to bookbinding to virtual reality. And her vociferous cat. She writes books that are fairly Black, usually queer, and very much embedded in the world of Sci-Fi, Fantasy & Horror.

MULTIMIND Publishing

Printed in the USA
CPSIA information can be obtained
at www.ICGtesting.com
CBHW021645050724
11140CB00013B/52

9 781952 860041